D1576939

The Rape of Tamar

Dan Jacobson's savagely funny and tragic
novel of the rape of King David's only
daughter by her brother Amnon

also by Dan Jacobson

The Trap
A Dance in the Sun
The Price of Diamonds
A Long Way from London
No Further West (*travel*)
The Evidence of Love
Time of Arrival
Beggar My Neighbour
The Beginners

WEIDENFELD AND NICOLSON 5 WINSLEY STREET LONDON W1

The Rape of Tamar

a novel by Dan Jacobson

Designed by Gerald Cinamon

Printed and made by C. Tinling & Co. Ltd,
London and Prescot

SBN 297 00155 8

I repeat – my memory is not loving but inimical,
and it labours not to reproduce but to distance the past.

Osip Mandelstam – *The Noise of Time*

1

Yes, I admit that the whole affair does have the look of a charade or costume-drama of some kind. Even to me. Is it simply because so many years have passed since the events took place, and fashions and habits have changed so greatly during that time? Or because the people involved in the story were themselves constantly aware of an audience looking to them for instruction and entertainment?

Probably both things apply. In any case, it's always difficult to take the dead quite seriously. What a dwarfish, slavish, disadvantaged race of spooks and less than spooks they are! If you choose not to think of them, they have no existence at all. If you do recall any one among them it is only to condemn him to go through a sequence of actions that, being dead, he can now never revise or modify. You may well wonder which is worse: to be forgotten, and hence utterly bereft of existence; or to be remembered solely in order to be driven again and yet again through one implacably unvarying routine, leading always to the same conclusion. If, *per impossibile*, the dead could choose, each would doubtless choose the state other to the one he is in: the remembered would choose to be forgotten, the forgotten to be remembered.

As for myself, I know only too well why I am remembered. I know the role I am condemned to play. I shall carry it out as conscientiously as I always do. Just watch.

So much by way of preamble. Now (and you may, if you wish, imagine me to be suitably dressed for my part, with my flesh and features arranged in a conventionally lifelike manner) allow me to introduce myself. My name is Yonadab.

Not a common name nowadays; at least in this part of the world. But some of you, a few of you, will have heard of me. I come from a most distinguished family.

You see, I can't pretend to be one of your anonymous narrators, one of your men in the street, one of your nondescript sons of the people. I am (or I was) the nephew of a king, the cousin of another, the uncle of a third. Ambitious men, all of them, hungry for power and position, eager for applause, determined to be remembered by generations following their own. And successful, too, at getting what they wanted. The name Yonadab may mean nothing to you; but you all know of David, Solomon, Absalom, and many others among my kinsmen.

However, please don't let these names overawe you. I'm sure that even the most plebeian among you will have little difficulty in recognising the conflicts and motives I'll have to speak of in the course of this narrative. In fact, if I sometimes feel embarrassed at the thought of how remote and archaic much of my story may appear to be, I am equally embarrassed at other times by how commonplace, how drearily familiar, you will find it all. Fraternal rivalries, incestuous desires, the struggles between a father and his sons, the greed for possessions and power ... The recollected dead are not the only ones who have to suffer the unending nausea of repetition.

But I anticipate. I had begun to introduce myself, and

8

must get back to that task. As I was saying, I am (or was) Yonadab: son of Shimeah, third son of Jesse, who was son of Obed, who was son of Boaz, who was son of Salma, who was son of Nachshon, 'prince of the tribe of Judah'. . . .

I shan't go on in that fashion, have no fear. I had enough of it when I was a child. My father was a great one for reciting the family pedigree. He found it comforting, apparently. I believe it made him feel that his place in the court of King David was one he held by right; that he was something more than a hanger-on, a client, a courtier, who had become what he was through a combination of chance and sycophancy. Yet, descendant from 'a prince of the tribe of Judah' though he may (or may not) have been, he was a true flunkey nevertheless; and he had all such a creature's natural resentments of his own position, and of the man who had given it to him. All and more. For to what you could call the ordinary humiliation of his position there was added that of having as his master someone who had once been his pushy little brother, the goat-herd of the family. Now the former goat-herd was king, and my father trembled at his angry looks. Literally. I saw it happen more than once. He trembled, trying to look imposing and dignified at the same time: a comic and disagreeable spectacle. No wonder that the resentment he had continually to swallow returned in the form of a slimy, yellow, acid stuff which he would belch up and spit out after almost every meal. Then he would smack his lips together and run his tongue over them, tasting the bitterness again. It was a good day for him when his eructations produced nothing but wind.

But I am not really tempted to sneer at his chronic indigestion, no matter how much its symptoms may have embarrassed and outraged me as a child. Besides, if I'm to belabour my father with your psychosomatic notions, I must be prepared to let the same rod fall on my own back. I had my health problems, too. Phlegm, in particular. Too many unspoken words, you could say, clogged my throat when I got out of bed every morning; clinging webs of frustration were spun within my chest while I slept, night after night. I don't suppose my children enjoyed my prolonged, matutinal throat-clearings, my cock-crow scrapings and garglings, any more than I had enjoyed my father's farts and belches.

Forgive me for bringing up these squalid domestic intimacies. Many of you must have expected quite another kind of introduction; one that would deal with much graver and broader issues. Something more political, perhaps. More historical. More religious. An outline, for example, of the most significant events that befell the kingdom and its people during David's reign. A description of the kingdom's physical features and of its economic resources. An account of the official religion of the state, and of the manner in which the religion was practised at various social levels. An analysis of the structure of our government, and of the division of duties between the king and his family, the judges and civil servants, the priesthood and the army.

All these are important matters. I shall have to touch on some of them later. Yet you must understand that I cannot come before you as an academic, would-be objective historian of a kind you are familiar with, and still less as an economist, political scientist, theologian, sociologist, or follower of any other of the learned disciplines that have become so fashionable among you in recent years. I have to be what I've always been. What that is (or was) disgusts me in many ways, I confess. Whenever I am compelled – how can I put it? – to experience my self yet again, whenever I have to endure my own consciousness once more, I find it intolerable that my interests and inclinations should be as low and limited as they are, so grovellingly personal in nature. But I cannot change them. My character is as unalterable now as my actions.

The living are supposed to have the advantage over me in that respect. Exercise it, I beg you, charitably. In return I can promise you that I shall do my very best to spare you extended descriptions of our exotic style of life: I don't intend to linger over our furniture, our clothes (broad vertical stripes in purple and white were very fashionable in my day, I might mention in passing), our utterly inadequate sewage systems, our weapons, our games, our primitive sacral rites, and all the rest of the ethnographical junk you may be glumly expecting me to inflict upon you. None of that is my business, either. I have only one job to do, one reason for being here.

I was speaking, then, before that last digression, about the rheumy frustrations and resentments that afflicted me; about the ambitions that I had been able to do nothing better with than turn into a plaguing catarrh. What were those ambitions? Can't you guess? Isn't it obvious? I wanted to be a king, that's all, a great general and leader of men, a terror to hosts of enemies, the master of innumerable women (and of a few obliging boys, too), the owner of palaces, stores of treasure, and great estates. Oh, and beautiful into the bargain, and a great musician and poet as well. But why go on? I wanted all the ordinary, banal, boring things that everyone wants. But I never came close to attaining any of my goals. From a very early age I was conscious of lacking one gift without which any others I may have possessed were useless. The gift I lacked was credulity.

David, the king, my uncle – to digress and anticipate once more – possessed it in abundance. His credulity was fierce, voracious, utterly unscrupulous. It brought him just about everything he could possibly have dreamed of when he herded his goats and sheep on the slopes of his father's ground outside Bethlehem. It hardly ever let him down. Until the day of his death he could believe – wholeheartedly, mind you, passionately, with an unfeigned zeal, with an absolutely intoxicating sense of righteousness and humility – practically anything that it suited him to believe. A gift of that order deserves the name of genius. Heaven knows, I don't underestimate his talents in other directions; far from it. But it was his credulity which was the sustaining and integrating principle of his character; it was his credulity that I always thought of as 'the secret of his success'.

Whereas scepticism was the secret of my failure. It's as good a formula as any. I utterly lacked the capacity to believe in the worth, or even the veracity, of anything I myself experienced. I am not boasting, you understand. I've always thought of my scepticism as a form of impotence, or as a kind of disease, a contagion or corruption which I carried around with me wherever I went, and which affected everything I saw or reflected upon. I never knew anyone in whom I was tempted for a moment to put an absolute trust, I was never able to commit myself wholly to an idea or a cause outside myself, my eye never failed to find the evidence it involuntarily sought of confusion and futility in every human enterprise. The world itself, to speak in the largest possible way, with all its heights, weights, colours, textures, wet places and dry, its wild and domestic beasts and plants of every kind, its myriads of insects and humans – this world has always seemed to me one about which it was quite impossible for me to come to any worthwhile conclusions whatsoever. Except that, in all its indifference and implausibility, it actually existed: it wasn't just an idea or image with which my mind or yours had somehow become lumbered. That such a world should be the creation of a deity or set of deities actively and intelligently concerned about its welfare, and about the moral comportment of its human inhabitants, always struck me, I need hardly add, as a self-evidently preposterous suggestion. I have never seen any reason to suppose that our interests and values have the slightest bearing upon the permanent, necessary workings of the world.

I leave it to you to decide whether the habit of mind which I have just described makes me a more or less reliable witness. As a way of bringing this much interrupted self-introduction to an end, however, I will ask you to imagine yourself to be ambitious and resentful of injury, as I was; to imagine that you have been brought up (the son of Shimeah, the flunkey) in a court full of intrigue and gossip; and to imagine yourself rabid with doubt about the value of every action you undertake or see others undertake. Now, what do you believe you will become? A philosopher? A misanthrope? A sensualist? A serene observer of the quarrels and feuds of others? Perhaps. I leave it to you, again, to decide for yourselves what I became.

2

My subject being what it is, my characters being what they are, I expect you would welcome a formal court scene before we go any further. Very well then, let us have one. Don't pitch your expectations too high, however. Remember that we are not culturally and technologically an advanced people. Our craftsmen are unskilled, our architecture is simple, our manners are crude. The kingdom itself has only been recently established, and therefore has not long been in a position to buy, pillage, or receive as tribute the treasures of its more sophisticated neighbours and predecessors. But we have done our best, and anything you may see of value and fine workmanship inside our houses, in any material from wood to gold, or from earthenware to lapis lazuli, is likely to be not 'ours' at all. All we have that we can really call our own are legends, tall stories, grandiose claims, the Name of our unnameable God.

Still, provincial and uncertain about the way to conduct ourselves though we may be, David does have a palace, and in that palace he does have a throne-room, and there, in the mornings, his sons, counsellors, commanders and priests are in the habit of gathering together around the king, while he transacts the business of the state; or at least that part of it which can be transacted in public. At these assemblies ordinary citizens present their petitions to him; he receives ambassadors and wealthy merchants from abroad; he announces decisions taken at more private meetings about taxation, say, or the call-up of new recruits and reservists into the militia; occasionally he passes sentence on convicted felons and traitors. One can say that these assemblies are a form of play-acting, for practically nothing takes place at them that has not been arranged beforehand; even the petitioners have been examined by the king's secretaries before they are allowed into his presence, and the king almost invariably follows the secretaries' advice in giving judgement on the pleas. Yet it is true that as far as the public is concerned, a decision taken by the king is not a decision until it has been declared; a gift is not a gift until it has been formally received; an appointment is not an appointment until it has been made known; a sentence is not a sentence until it has been pronounced.

Anyway, the king enjoys the assemblies. Therefore, we all do, or pretend we do; play-acting pleasure at play-acting solemnity. We stand about in our groups, in no regular order and in no prescribed places; none of us turns his back on the king, however, and none of us speaks unless he has signified to us that we may do so. You may imagine that the room is rather long and narrow; its walls are plastered in alternating panels of dark blue, ochre, and white; its ceiling, supported by square pillars, is coffered in gilded wood; its floor is of stone; the only item of furniture in it is the king's throne, an elaborate ivory-sheathed affair that had once been sat upon, no doubt, by a Canaanite princeling. Curtains hang across the wide doorway at the far end of the room; and around them peep various members of the public who have managed to talk the guards into letting them see some of the splendours of the place.

We also are among the splendours at which they have come to stare, and of course we are conscious of their presence, though we pretend not to be. This is especially true of our leading performers, our major figures, our stars. They are so famous that the goggling outsiders look at them, just as you do, with incredulity, surprise and a certain gasp of – yes, of amusement, an instinctive impulse to laughter, as if to say: How dare they –? How dare they claim to be what they are? There is the king, with his small, bright, high-coloured, grey-bearded face, his hands energetically clasping the arms of the throne, like a man about to rise at any moment. There is his eldest son, Amnon, my 'best friend' in the court, and the hero, villain, and tragic clown of my story; he stands aside, a sulky look on his face, making no pretence at being pleased to be in the room. There is Absalom; he too is detached,

15

and his lips are curved in that faint, unconscious, abstracted smile that extremely handsome men often wear. Now Solomon stands next to the throne, and allows his father to stroke the silky lobes of his ears, his eyes big not with the pleasure he is getting but with the pleasure he knows he is giving. His brother, Adonijah, who will one day be killed at the orders of that obliging little boy (grown by then into a plump, calculating, self-indulgent young man), looks on indifferently, shifting his weight from one strong leg to the other. My father stifles a belch. No one is armed, except for the soldiers of the king's guard who stand at the door and immediately behind his throne, and the most senior army officers who happen to be present.

Statements are made, greetings are exchanged, documents are read out, the petitioners talk in faltering voices, they bow, weep, babble, are escorted out when the king has had enough of them. The ache in our feet reminds us that we are underlings. So be it. At last the king stands and makes his way out of the room, his bodyguard preceding him. After such meetings he almost always goes to the women's quarters of the palace, where he can relax, where he takes an early luncheon. Usually he invites some of the company to follow him; I shall see to it that you will join such a group soon. The rest of us remain in the throne-room for a while, gossiping, discussing what we have just seen and heard, making conversation with the visitors from abroad or officials from the provinces who have come to the capital to present their reports to one or another of the councils. For a few minutes our gestures are a little freer, our laughter and talk a little louder, than they usually are, now that we are rid of the restraint imposed on us by the king's presence. It could be said that we make a positive display of being at ease, the better to impress the gaping onlookers at the doors. Then we begin to drift out, some of us to carry out the work that will lead to a precisely similar meeting the next day, and the day after that; others to follow the example of the king and take our midday meal. The show is over.

Yet what a strange show it is, all said and done: this drama whose very point it almost invariably is that there should be no drama; whose purpose is to demonstrate how smoothly the machinery of the state functions, how promptly and unquestioningly the king's orders are obeyed. We have just participated in a ritual, if you like, which accumulates tension in order to disperse it – or rather, in order to show that there is no need for tension. Therefore you may be sure that the king is wily enough to see to it that in days of peace like those which we now enjoy, the ritual is from time to time interrupted by a sudden change of mind on his part, or an outburst of rage, or an announcement that no one expects. Thus the effect of the show on other days is made so much the more compelling.

The tricks of the governing trade. Is there one that David doesn't know and employ when it suits him? He is inexhaustible. Even the bareness of his throne-room is one of his tricks: you are expected to be moved by what it reveals of his simplicity, intimidated by what it reveals of his earnestness of purpose. He is a master of surprise and duplicity; gentle when you expect him to be stern, savage when you expect him to be indulgent, unbending when you expect him to be relaxed, familiar when you expect him to be aloof. And that's not all; not by any means. You must admit, for example, that it's not a small achievement to have your enemies killed off by your henchmen, as any other tyrant would, and then to win for yourself a reputation as a man of honour and tender conscience – how? By killing, in a fit of outraged sensibility, those who have done the job for you! Yet David has pulled off that particular trick more than once; and will try to do something very much like it again even from his death-bed. Who but David could employ butchers like Joab and Abishai as his commanders and executioners; yet go around the palace sighing and wringing his hands over their ruthlessness? Who can weep hotter tears or deliver a more impassioned eulogy than David over an enemy who is safely dead? And that's not all, either.

But I insist: I am not accusing David of hypocrisy. On the contrary, I am accusing him of sincerity. If we in the palace, hardened professionals, were constantly abashed by the brilliant, unflawed purity of that conscience of his, you can imagine the effect it had on the populace. Consider also the effect it must have had on his sons. Especially as he made a point of being unfailingly generous towards them, giving them houses, farmlands, flocks, servants, women, titles, everything they asked for. Except power. Except the satisfaction of knowing where they stood with him. Except freedom from his insatiable demand for love and admiration.

Shadows of shadows. Words from a vanished mouth. The way David and his court went through that formal little performance of theirs a moment ago, you'd think I really was King Yonadab (at last!). Instead – well, you know who I am. Having meddled and interfered as much as I dared with David and his people when they were rather more than shadows, I am now condemned to be a stage-manager to phantoms; an annalist (analyst?) of apparitions; a spook-spokesman. Not a fate I can be entirely serious about.

So allow me to call on various members of the court to assemble around the king once more, informally this time, in a smaller room elsewhere in the palace. Let it be the same day or another. Amnon still stands aside, passing sulky judgement on the people around him. His thick lips are pursed forward, a little of the pink flesh inside exposed. (After his death, Amnon's lips will hold fast in that characteristic pout a morsel of his own dried blood.) Standing there, he might be thought to be angry; it's certain that he's unhappy. Whenever the king's gaze falls on him he moves uneasily, his black lashes flicker. When they talk about domestic or foreign politics, Amnon accuses them, usually silently but sometimes aloud, of being greedy, bloody, obsessed with power, crazy for possessions and an unreal glory. When they gossip together about common acquaintances, Amnon accuses them of revealing the basic triviality and frivolity of their minds. When they talk about religious services or the celebration of festivals, Amnon accuses them of superstition and obscurantism. When they talk about Amnon, the blood rises under the dark skin of his cheeks, even his forehead darkens, beneath his combed, oiled, jet-black hair.

'There's no pleasing Amnon,' the king says.

Everyone smiles discreetly. Amnon has made many enemies: inevitably, his nature being what it is. So some feel only gratification at seeing him discomfited. Others are a little sorry for him, for they know that if Amnon's nature afflicts them, it afflicts him even more.

Or the king says, turning from side to side with an air of utter simplicity and frankness, his hands apart, palms upward, 'What does he want? What *does* he want?'

Nobody dares to reply. We shuffle our feet, we exchange glances with one another, we wait for the king to move on to another subject. The king's sons are even more subdued and non-committal, perhaps, than the courtiers. For several reasons. In the first place, none of them knows when it mightn't be his turn to find himself the unhappy victim of his father's simplicity and bewildered frankness. In the second place, their father disapproves violently of any of them ever showing the slightest sign of what he, David, would call disloyalty to one another. He is always ready to tell them that they must live together as true friends and comrades, begrudging one another nothing; they are all his sons, all equally dear to him, all the source of his deepest pride; and as they are to him so they should be to one another. On the whole, the brothers try to avoid giving him the opportunity of unleashing his eloquence on the subject.

So it's left to Amnon to reply, if he so chooses. When he does, his answers are usually brief, obscure, and untruthful. 'I just want to be left alone,' he says. Or, 'I just want to be a good son to you, that's all'. Or, 'There's nothing you can give me that I want, nothing at all'. David at once answers with further questions. 'Then why do you look at me so reproachfully? Why do you come here if you really want to be left alone? But you are a good son to me, aren't you?' And so on. Perfectly fair and reasonable questions. Which is the worst thing you can say about them, the impasse between the two men being what it is.

Of course, we all have our own particular, prized insights into the impasse; we have all speculated about 'how it will all end'. But none of us ever expects it to come to its 'end' on any one of the occasions that we are compelled to witness. Besides, there are all the other times when Amnon doesn't stand apart at all. When he is in a different, rarer mood, hardly a subject comes up for discussion about which he doesn't express his opinions: hectoringly, earnestly, with a great readiness to take offence if everyone doesn't agree with them. At these times David listens, smiles, lowers his chin as if in embarrassment, and looks up at no one in particular through the thick, tufted, greying brows that sit so oddly (yes, you could easily take them to be false ones!) on his narrow face. It is clear that he thinks as little of Amnon's bouts of loquacity as he does of his silences; but he responds in a manner that, though we have seen it many times before, never fails to surprise us. He eggs Amnon on, he encourages him by pretending to take him seriously, or by pretending to differ from him only on minor points, or by capping Amnon's notions with even more extravagant ideas of his own. It is the closest they ever come to being in harmony with one another, these two strange men, when they are playing together in this way (though one of them doesn't know that that is what they are doing). Amnon is excited, he wags his head like a bull, on his face there is a slightly astonished, foolish expression of challenge and gratification; David appears positively to enjoy the scorn he inwardly feels towards his first-born son. His pleasure is so private, so intimate, you might think Amnon is a phase or stage in his own life left so far behind him that he can now look back on it without anger or humiliation, but with amusement, merely. Furthermore, to make the comedy more complete, it is during these outbursts that Amnon reveals the depth of his father's influence over him in ways of which neither he nor David is in the least aware. Though Amnon is not at all like his father in appearance, he nevertheless imitates his father's gestures, facial movements, and intonations of voice, as if engaged in a ponderous, self-communing parody of his own.

Bastards aside, there are nineteen princes, nineteen sons of the king, in the court, ranging in age from Amnon in his middle twenties to little Eliphelet who is barely out of his napkins. They range enormously in talent and temperament, too: one is excellent at handling animals; another is devout; a third is subject to attacks of *petit mal*, during which he puts his nodding head to one side, closes his eyes, and chews mildly on his tongue; Chileab is so myopic there is no prospect of him ever attaining to the throne. By right, Amnon, being the oldest son, should be their leader, but though this is a position he noisily claims for himself from time to time, none of the others ever really grants it to him. If anything, they are inclined to use him as a butt for some of their sillier pranks; they enjoy teasing him and making him lose his temper over trivialities. Why should they follow Amnon, when each of them hopes that the others will one day follow him? For it goes without saying that the brothers are extremely jealous of one another's privileges, despite (or perhaps in part because of) David's sermons on the subject.

Indeed, there are many occasions when I suspect David of knowing this perfectly well, and of moralising at them at such length in order to humiliate them, to drive them apart from one another, to try to make sure that they won't unite against him. From one aspect, which David likes to dwell upon in public, these boys are his own legendary youth and life renewed. From another, which you may be sure he is self-conscious and dark-minded enough to be aware of, his sons are nothing less than his supplanters, even perhaps his murderers. They carry the sign of his death between their unlined brows; their strong young arms threaten him with it; they will walk on his grave with those sturdy legs of theirs.

But I don't want to make things sound more sombre than they really are. The court would be a dull place without the princes. They are always organising theatrical performances, races on foot and horseback, military exercises and parades, elaborate dinner parties; they carry out practical jokes on people they don't like; they disrupt some of the most holy ceremonies of the calendar by getting unspeakable, torturing fits of the giggles when they catch one another's eyes at inopportune moments; they go on mad expeditions into the desert and come back with trophies of dubious value – strangely veined rocks, small Bedouin boys strayed from their encampments, species of addax and desert rat which they claim have never before been seen by civilised man.

Such are the pastimes of peace. Decades have passed since the king succeeded in uniting Israel and Judah, the warring northern and southern halves of his kingdom; years since any of our neighbours have challenged the hegemony which he established over them in many bloody, well-remembered battles. The great powers of Egypt, Mesopotamia, and Asia Minor remain in a state of decline and disarray, incapable of exerting any political influence within the area, let alone of sending out forces to subjugate it. We control the lucrative trade east and west between the Mediterranean and the Red Sea, north and south between Phoenicia and Egypt. Our subject peoples pave roads for the traders to travel on, and build forts for our protection; their upper classes are glad to take up appointments in the service of the state and to marry their daughters to our officers; the Cherethites and Pelethites, once the allies of the Philistines, now make up the members of the king's bodyguard, in rotation; our farmers till their fields and orchards, and build their terraces; craftsmen and masons of all nationalities flock to Jerusalem to help build and beautify the city.

The king resides in his capital, which has become the symbol of the unity of the country he can be said to have created. Occasionally, however, he goes on a royal progress through one or another of the provinces of his kingdom: he visits the towns along the coastal plain, or the hills and lakes of Galilee; he crosses the wilderness to Jericho, or goes south, to Hebron and beyond, into the deserts where he had once lurked as a young man, and gathered his forces around him, and played off Philistine against Israelite, and Judaean against both, shedding blood, fleeing, and coming back again, like any other bandit or guerilla chieftain. Now at every town and settlement he is greeted by his governors, local dignitaries, priests and officers of his garrisons. They hold parades for him to inspect, they have prepared sacrifices at their holy places for him to carry out; he reviews their arrangements and distributes praise and rebuke as he sees fit. Then he departs. The long caravan of chariots and wagons sways and jolts between the stony hills and across the narrow valleys which make up so much of the country; the small boys running alongside at last grow footsore and drop behind, though they still look on longingly, their hands shielding their eyes from the sun; the weapons and armour of the accompanying troops flash in the distance; the trumpets fall silent until the next town draws near.

Picturesque, isn't it? Uncomfortable, too. Especially for a man who is no longer young; who in fact is growing old. The shaking and jolting over rutted paths, the heat and dust in summer and the mud and cold in winter, the ill-prepared, provincial banquets for which he has so little appetite, the gaping of crowds and the noise they make – all things considered, it isn't surprising that the king makes these progresses more and more reluctantly; that he now leaves the capital only once or twice a year at most, and instead sends others to deputise for him as often as he can. Now he sends Amnon, now Absalom, now groping

Chileab, or Adonijah. He sends Ira, his chief minister and the most devoted of his civil servants, who hates the job, or his chief priests, Abiathar and Zadok, who do their best; he even sends my father who goes off with such turkey-cock swellings that out of sheer charity (rather than shame) I forbear to dwell on them.

The truth is that the king, of whose strengths only I have so far spoken, has begun to show his years. He is becoming increasingly erratic, lachrymose, given to endless reminiscences about his feats as a young man, all of which we have heard many times before (and which his scribes write down or pretend to write down every time he bids them do so). Every now and again he is still capable of displaying such agility of mind that one is forced to suspect him of using his age as a kind of disguise, as just another one of his subterfuges. But it isn't so; he is not what he was; and he realises it anew, perhaps, every time he gathers his sons around him and tells them again just how much he loves them and how important it is that they should put their love for one another above every other consideration.

Peace, and an ageing king: a dangerous combination of circumstances. It is bound to lead to boredom, dissatisfaction, a conviction that all existing social arrangements are an affront to the energy and power of youth. There are many young men around David who, listening to his stories of his own youth, are ready to see themselves as so many young Davids, and David as a feeble, contemptible Saul. Moreover – and this is in part due to the extent of David's astonishing military, political, and religious success – the ambitions of the young are given a particular urgency by the feeling, widespread among us, that we are utterly unlike those undistinguished, anonymous ancestors of ours who worked themselves miserably

25

into the earth to no purpose at all; that we are living in the very time of times, the one towards which history has always been labouring, the only real time our race has known, as against all the meaningless times that are past.

And now look at me! And look at you! No wonder each of us thinks that the laugh is on the other.

With his flunkey's nose for power and esteem, my father disapproved strongly of my friendship with Amnon. Amnon just didn't smell like a success to him. So what, he wanted to know, did I see in him? Did I really enjoy his company? Didn't I realise that by being known in the court as Amnon's crony I was perhaps damaging my future position? Not to speak of his own, Shimeah's? Didn't I find Amnon's quarrelsomeness and unreliability impossible to tolerate?

Well, yes. I did find Amnon impossible at times. I told my father so, too. But I also used to tell him that Amnon amused me, which was true; that I didn't care about my position in the court, which was rather less true; and that in any case, one didn't choose one's friends in order to secure advancement, did one?

No, no, answered my father, who had never done anything else, shocked at the suggestion; he opened his eyes wide and shook his head so hard that his flabby cheeks shook too, to demonstrate his piety before the idea of selfless, disinterested friendship. But still – still –

I knew what he meant by that 'Still – '. He was right to be puzzled by my friendship with Amnon. I was often puzzled by it myself. It wasn't easy being Amnon's best friend. I don't know whether it was more difficult when he was all over me with his protestations of undying regard, or when he refused to speak to me for weeks on end. Yet amusement, curiosity, and what I can only call an instinct for calamity kept me from abandoning him. And you can't say that Amnon let me down in the end! I was to have my reward for all the days I spent out in the fields with him, riding or hunting with dogs; the dinners and parties at which he boozed, gambled, sang songs, and practised feats of strength with young army officers or layabouts who had been sent by their parents to get what they could out of the court; the summer nights on the roof of his house, when I would lie on my back, on some rugs, bemused by the brightness of the stars overhead, while Amnon talked, talked, talked incessantly.

What about? His grievances, mostly. Any topic about which Amnon went on for long enough was likely to turn into a grievance. I would fall into a doze, wake and agree with him, drowse again. Night after night the jackals in the hills outside the city kept up an energetic, mirthless jubilation that occasionally guttered away into chuckles and then rose into a renewed chorus of prolonged, competitive shrieks. You might have thought they were being paid to do it. The dogs of the town, out on their own scavenging missions, answered bluffly, bravely, without conviction. For the rest, the lanes and alleyways of the city would be quiet; few lamps or fires would still be burning anywhere, even along the walls of the palace, higher up the hill. Many times, in the course of his monologues, Amnon shook his fist in that direction. His father, his brothers (Absalom especially), the condition of the kingdom, his dissatisfaction with his own looks, his thieving servants – there was no end to the subjects he was ready to conduct his monologues on.

But of Tamar, his sister, he did not speak at all until the night on which I suppose it can be said our story properly begins (and about time too!). The stars flickered, the jackals howled, the dogs barked, and Amnon wandered restlessly about the roof, now leaning against the parapet, now standing over me and staring down, but never saying a word. Instead, he sighed and groaned, clenched a fist and punched it against his open palm, muttered sounds of no meaning, and went off again on his prowlings about the terrace. The movements of his pale robes were far more impassioned than anything I could make out of his face. I hadn't seen him for a few weeks: he had avoided everyone, locking himself in his house, sinking himself into what everyone assumed was just another of his famous 'moods'. Then he had sent a messenger to me, asking me to come to him, to come at once. But I hadn't yet learned why; all I had seen, when I had entered the house, was that he looked ill, unkempt, and much thinner than before. I waited for him to explain his agitation. Waiting, I fell asleep.

When I awoke I knew at once that I had been asleep for hours; it was that time of night when you feel by a thinning and chilling of the air in your lungs, rather than by any change in the intensity of the darkness, that dawn is approaching. Amnon was crouching in a corner of the roof, his back against the parapet. Had he fallen asleep like that? No, he was awake, his head was moving too sharply for him not to have been conscious; he looked as if he were arguing with himself. Still? I lay down again. I heard secretive, deglutitious noises, almost like a man shamefacedly eating something. Only then did I become aware that the dogs and jackals had fallen silent. Not even a cock crowed. But Amnon was sobbing.

He must have seen or sensed that I had woken. He came over to me and dropped on his knees by my side, taking my wrist in a fierce grip. He smelled stale, dyspeptic.

'Can I trust you?' he cries and wheezed, his shoulders shaking. 'Are you my brother? Will you be my brother, my real brother, not like all the rest of them? Do you swear that you are?'

'What is it, Amnon? What do you want? What's the matter?'

He didn't answer my questions. Instead, between gasps, he began rambling incoherently about a blood-brotherhood ceremony he wanted the two of us to go through. We would cut our arms and mingle our blood. We would kill a goat. Exchange weapons. Bury a gold ring. Recite holy spells he had been taught by a magician, an Edomite magician. I wanted to laugh out loud. Was it for the sake of this dreary rubbish that he had watched the night through? Sighed, sobbed, paced up and down? There was an insane combination of fervour and distraction in his voice, as if he himself couldn't believe in the importance of what he was saying.

In the end I agreed to go through the ceremony. He said he wanted it; he could have it. What did I have to lose? At once he stood up. I thought he was going to start the hocus-pocus right then. But he backed away silently, wringing his hands in front of his chest. He stood across the roof from me and began to recite in a trembling voice something that wasn't a spell or a benediction at all, but a law, a prohibition; to him it must have sounded like a curse. It was the law forbidding a man, on pain of death, 'to uncover', as the archaic language of the statute put it, 'the nakedness of his sister'.

I was still at a loss, utterly uncomprehending. What kind of priest or lawgiver did he imagine he'd become? What was he accusing me of? Then, suddenly and completely, though he said no more, I understood. No wonder his mind was running on occult and unnatural forms of brotherhood! I was the first to utter her name; I knew it must be her.

'Tamar!'

Only then was he set free to say the name too; its second syllable became no more than a sad, prolonged vibration within the husk of his mouth.

He turned and ran, he scuttled away downstairs like a guilty schoolboy. Somehow, it was that pathetic, furtive scuttle of his, rather than all the tears and groans I had heard before, which made me suspect that the calamity I'd always anticipated might at last be truly upon him.

Incidentally, Amnon and I never did go through that blood-brotherhood ritual of his. During the days and weeks that followed he continued to speak of it, but he put off carrying it out, put it off again, mentioned it less often, ceased to mention it at all. Probably he felt it had become pointless to pursue the matter, seeing that he had already taken me into his confidence. It makes no difference. I would have betrayed him anyway.

3

It really is very ironic. Ambitious people are those who are determined to secure for themselves exemption from the humiliations and misfortunes that others simply have to endure as best they can. Yet once the ambitious have achieved power and position, they and their families become more, not less, exposed to temptation, to error, to disastrous reversals of fortune. Hence, in the end, all they succeed in turning themselves into are great exemplars of the ordinary, overwhelming instances of the commonplace. Look at my cousin, Amnon! Ordinary men who begin to burn and shiver with desire for their closest female relations are usually compelled to find the best release their own busy fingers under the bedclothes can bring them. But the very powerful are in a position to take greater risks. 'What's the point of being a prince if you can't do it?' I said to Amnon at one stage, after he had confessed his secret to me. Whereupon he replied, as if all those wretches with their hands under the bedclothes had their eyes fixed only on him, 'What's the point of being a prince if I do?'

Exactly. It was a good reply, I had to admit. Better than I would have thought Amnon capable of making. Even though I did find something comical, at the same time, in the idea of Amnon solemnly trying to put himself forward as a model of self-restraint and high-mindedness, as a being uncontaminated by the filthy desires of the mass of mankind. Amnon? The same man who in other moods made such a point of impressing on me how irresistible was the passion that drove him; of begging me to realise that he could no more be blamed for what he felt than an epileptic could be blamed for rolling on the ground in the midst of his seizure. He was gripped by illness, madness, fate . . .

It was all very impressive. I was most impressed. I still am, whenever I have to recall his cries and ejaculations on the subject. Also, I must acknowledge that Tamar did indeed turn out to be his fate; he wasn't exaggerating at all in calling her that. Just as he, in a different way, turned out to be hers. However, my scepticism compels me to add that once Amnon had allowed himself to set his eyes on the girl, the only possibilities open to him were either to exercise complete self-restraint or to start talking about madness and fate and all the rest of it. What other justification could he offer her, or himself, or anyone else? No, it had to be love, true love, overmastering love, all-devouring love. The works. Or nothing.

What a choice. What a pair of alternatives. Especially to someone like Amnon, who had been given more and more reason to suppose that nothing was just what he was cut out to be. Nothing in the eyes of his father; nothing in the eyes of his brothers; nothing in the eyes of the rest of the court; nothing in the eyes of that God or those gods in whose powers he intermittently believed. You don't think him capable of such self-knowledge? If so, the fault is mine; I haven't been fair in what I've shown you of him. Despite his singularities, Amnon was not so different, I assure you, from you and me; and just like the rest of us he carried around with him certain uneasy, recurring apprehensions of his own worthlessness, his own absolute inconsequence. But being the son of a king, the possible heir to a kingdom, and a young man of many baffled passions and ambitions, he also had unusually bold ideas of the power and importance that could be his if only he dared to be more than nothing.

For it wasn't just as an exemplar of self-restraint to the swinish masses that Amnon could picture himself. There were other obvious possibilities open to him; other examples he could follow, or set. Near enough to us, both historically and geographically, were those Egyptian kings, divine themselves, whose brides were transformed into their divine sisters upon ascending to the royal bed. Nearer to us still were Anat, of our own land of Canaan, and her brother-husband, Baal: Baal the fructifier and life-giver, and Anat the ambitious, hard-working, scheming and miraculously virginal goddess to whom, in all honest confusion, so many of our people prayed, and whose potbellied figurine, sexual organs prominently displayed, was to be found on so many of our hearths. Tamar-Anat, Amnon-Baal. . . . Why not? If the son and daughter of a king broke the laws, or went beyond them, then surely anything could be possible: new laws or no laws, another life, a share in eternity, the banishment of death. Who could tell? Not Amnon. And how could Amnon, of all people, forget that Baal and Anat, according to some legends were in a state of indecisive, continuous rebellion against the older, higher, dimmer paternal god, El? The same story again! Always the same damn story; the same incitements, opportunities, and compulsions.

After all of which I fear you will be disappointed (yet again) when I introduce you to Tamar. A goddess? An instrument of fate and doom? She hardly looks it. She is much too young, too slight, too simple in appearance. If you wanted to be kind and patronising you might think of her as 'a pretty little thing'. If you wanted to be dismissive (and somewhat out-of-date in your idiom) you could call her 'a slip of a girl'. If you wanted to be nasty you could say that she is 'a spoiled little brat'.

Oval eyes, a sallow complexion, lips that are full and have a faintly bluish or purple tint. A lithe, immature body, concealed and revealed by the robes she wears. Thin wrists. A small foot. Gold ornaments in her hair and around her childish neck. A curiously stealthy, undulating walk. An air of gravity that isn't really accounted for by anything she ever says, or by any emotion she ever shows. What else? A habit of holding her head quite still when she speaks, the effect being a little theatrical, as if she is delivering something learned off by heart. There she is then, as best as I can briefly describe her: Tamar, daughter of David and his late consort Ma'acah, who had herself been daughter of the so-called 'King of Geshur'; sister to Absalom; half-sister to Amnon and all the other princes.

David adores her. Though he has other daughters, to whom he pays no attention, by his concubines, Tamar is his only daughter by one of his official wives. So he thinks of her as his only daughter, he calls her his only daughter; and he loves her with all the weakness and storm of his many-sided heart. Solomon apart, there is no child of his who is as much petted and to whom so much is permitted. When she was a child he was always dandling and nuzzling her; now that she is a young woman he merely watches her with a regard that is wondering, attentive, kindly, a little pathetic in its combination of awareness and incomprehension, experience and helplessness. In a curious way his regard is detached, almost impersonal; one feels that every time he looks at her he has to acknowledge that his own overweening personality has its limits, and that these are not the limits of the world either. It is striking, too, that though the king has become so much more garrulous as he has grown older, he is generally rather silent in Tamar's company. He listens carefully when she speaks to him, and accedes readily enough to any request she makes of him; but his reticence nevertheless creates an area of stillness around the two of them which the rest of us are careful not to intrude upon. We hold our breath, so to speak, whenever they are together; it sometimes shocks us that Tamar does not do so as well.

Instead, and inevitably perhaps, she takes her position in the regard of the king quite for granted. She has a calm, unquestioning belief in her own importance that would make her insufferable if she weren't also rather an obliging girl on the whole, usually eager to be approved of, and much impressed by the prowess of her father and all her brothers. If she lacks humour – well, she doesn't need it. If she loses her temper sometimes it is never with her father or her brothers, but only with the servants and other women of the royal household, and she makes her complaints about them to the king in the most charming manner: widening her eyes and dropping (not raising) her voice, as if she finds it quite incredible that anyone should be intentionally disobliging to her. That drop of her voice, it is plain, delights the king, it is enough to make him infirm with tenderness and amusement. Tamar, of course, knows it. She imagines that she knows everything she will ever really need to know.

As you see, my tone about her is cool. I prefer that it should be so; for if it weren't, it would be intemperate. Christ! – if I may call on the name of the most famous of my family connections – that these creatures, these young girls, should have the power over us that they do! Just because they have smaller bones than our own, softer skins, clearer eyes; because they have slender hips that are wider, all the same, than their sloping shoulders; because they move their arms this way, turn their heads that way, draw breath in such a rhythm, lean forward or back with so many other crossings of curves, hollows and inclinations. What trifling causes to produce such terrible consequences: filling us with yearning and exaltation, driving us to fight, hold, clutch, fuck, making us imagine that here – there – now – again – we will find surcease from all the hungers and uncertainties that plague us. From girls like Tamar who, in short, are quite unremarkable in every respect.

Harassed, let's say, by these seditious or at any rate resentful thoughts, I break my bread and reach into the bowl of mutton stew that stands in the middle of the table, while the king, always a sparse eater and drinker, reclines on a couch and looks with satisfaction on the heartiness of his sons' appetites. Tamar and Bathsheba, his favourite wife, sit at the table too; something that the king permits only within the privacy of the family circle. Tamar eats languidly, with long pauses between each mouthful; her stool is at the foot of David's couch, and thus near the head of the table; she is half-turned towards her father, and I am able to see her from the side only. You may take it that the room we are in is one of the most sumptuously furnished and decorated you are likely to see in the palace. Its walls are gaily painted in the Egyptian style, with birds and beasts emerging from clumps and thickets of broad-bladed foliage; tables and chairs are heavily and ornately inlaid with brass; the king's vessels are of repoussé gold and silver, and ours of alabaster. We are waited upon by young boys and old women, while the major-domo stands at the door, his posture and the look on his face as stupid and self-important as those of all fat head-waiters at all times.

Fruit. Wine. Small cakes dipped in honey. Bowls of water in which to wash our hands. We are replete. The kingdom is at peace, and for the moment so are we. It is evident to all of us that we deserve our good fortune: our position in the court, our decorated room, our handsome tableware, the food we have just eaten. The king beckons to the musician who has been standing to one side, ready to play if he should be asked to do so, and the man hastens over and drops on his knees before his master. David takes the lyre from him and tunes it. His expression is sly, dreamy, somehow a little ashamed of his own skill with the instrument yet complacently certain that we will be gratified by his condescension in playing for us, for he is known to do it only when he is in an excellent humour. He plucks a tune from the seven strings, his head lowered, his thin, young-looking fingers working strongly yet tremulously among them.

He looks up as the last note hums its way into silence. None of us would dare to applaud, but we all try to look as though no applause could ever do justice to the ineffable aesthetic experience we have just enjoyed.

'Come, Tamar,' the king says. 'I'll play, and you'll sing.'

Tamar considers for a moment, then shakes her head. Her refusal isn't pert; merely disinclined, idle.

'That's not very kind of you. We would all enjoy it.'

'I wouldn't.'

'Ah, that's just what you say now – '

The king is begging her. To no avail. Tamar looks around the table, without confusion or embarrassment; if anyone is embarrassed it is the king. Bathsheba says reprovingly, 'Tamar!' and for her pains earns a glare from the king. He calls the musician over once again, and hands the lyre back to him.

'No, I do understand,' he says eventually, with some effort, as if answering a comment none of us has made. 'I know how Tamar feels. If you have talent people imagine that it's easy for you to make use of it whenever you're asked to do so. But it isn't easy at all.' With every phrase he visibly feels a little better, the words come more freely; he is turning the incident more and more to Tamar's advantage, and hence to his own as well. Instead of having witnessed a bit of impertinence on her part, you understand, we have been privileged to gain an insight into the temperament of the artist; a temperament which only David can truly understand and sympathise with, being blessed or cursed with it himself. Soon he will be quite warm on the subject.

But Tamar interrupts him by rising and taking a few steps back from the table so that she stands almost against the wall. She bows her head deeply to him in a gesture of submission, clasping her hands together at her waist. She waits until everyone has finished turning on his stool to see her and has fallen silent. The king gives her a measured nod of approval before looking satisfiedly around the table; from his expression you would think Tamar has now not only vindicated completely what he was saying, but has also demonstrated the depth of her obedience to him. Then she opens her lips and begins to sing, unaccompanied.

Her voice is small, but pleasing; the song is simple, and makes no demands of her which she cannot meet; the words are familiar to us all. A young girl, a stern father, a poor young wooer who has neither metal nor flocks but only his strength and beauty to offer, an ambush, a death, a suicide. Tamar draws a deep breath into her chest between each verse, a lesser breath at the end of each line. A tiny flicker or contraction of her brow warns us that she has lost a phrase; a glance of reassurance at her father before her lips and tongue utter it shows us that she has found it again.

David has not taken his eyes off her since the song began. Absalom, too, has been watching her closely. He is obviously touched by the delicacy and sweetness of her appearance, by the fragility of her voice, even perhaps by the trite words of the song she is singing; he is anxious, as any loving brother might be, that she should acquit herself well. Yet the approving tilt of his head suggests that in her performance, and in what went before it, he has been confirmed in his belief that the children of

Ma'acah will always be the recipients of special favours, that they will always be set apart for good reasons from the other members of the Royal Family.

Hi'la, hi'na, hi'lalala
Yi'la, yi'na, yi'lalala

For the last time Tamar repeats the meaningless, melancholy refrain of the song. Then she returns to her stool, while we applaud. A pleasant domestic scene. However, as you have doubtless guessed, I haven't described it at such length for its own sweet sake, but because it was at that moment, according to Amnon, or at one so much like it as to make no difference, that 'it' happened to him; that his madness began; that he saw Tamar for what she would henceforth be to him.

Whether Amnon was telling the truth in saying this is something I can't vouch for. I simply don't know whether or not you should believe his talk about the softness and warmth he felt beneath her dress when she brushed past him on her way back to her stool; about the scent from her hair that suddenly filled his nostrils; about the glimpse he had of a small, curved hand and its polished fingernails resting against his tunic. He may have been lying. For all I know, he may, without ever having told me of it, have cherished lustful thoughts about her ever since his childhood; when they were children he may already have fingered her beneath beds and behind curtains, gathering dust and guilt together. I don't know. And except for what it reveals about his own festering state of mind, I certainly wouldn't attach any importance to his claim that it was partly because of the way David and Absalom had looked at the girl that he found himself possessed by desire for her. That, seeing how they looked at her, he realised, however inarticulately, the power he might be able to exercise over them through Tamar: yes, it seems plausible enough. But that they were lusting after her, that they were looking at her with 'goats' eyes' (to use his words): no, that's pure Amnon, pure guilt, pure confusion. You would have to be Amnon himself to believe it; and even then you'd probably have difficulty at times.

Anyway, he always stuck to his story. Always the passion came to him from nowhere, from everywhere: from a glint in his father's moist eye, from the sound of a drawn breath, from the upraised beak of a bird on the mural, from a flicker of light off a goblet of wine, from a soft pressure against his shoulder. For some minutes he is stifled, uncomprehending, there is a pressure in his ears, he stares at an apple-core on his plate, a gnawn, scraggy thing in which brown seeds nestle, each in its own split, smooth-textured pod. He does not think of Tamar, he does not think at all; his mind is empty. Then understanding returns to him, but as if it too were a physical sensation: he feels it pass through his head, from an unknown centre within him, moving outwards in a single pang, gathering strength, growing ever more sharp and blade-like, until he is being split from within, his breast and forehead are cleaved with an exquisite pain, still moving out of himself. He will fall, he will faint, he will lie shattered and split.

Instead he finds himself on his feet. He has uttered two words, only two, but for the moment they have saved him from that knife-blade within. 'Tamar!' he has said; and, 'No!'

'Didn't you see me stand up?' he asked me, later. 'Didn't you see how I looked around?'

I had to admit that I hadn't noticed him doing so. It was possible he had; but the meal, always informal, was at its end; others may have stood up at the same time, or just after. How could I tell?

'Ach!' Amnon replied, with disgust at my impercipience. He had stood there like a drunk, for minutes on end, looking vaguely around him, looking everywhere but at Tamar. And I hadn't seen him? But perhaps it had only seemed to him that minutes were passing: perhaps that was why I hadn't noticed him. He may have stood at his place for a few seconds only, the slowest he had ever endured. While they lasted he knew with perfect clarity and simplicity all that was later to become confused within him, labyrinthine, hopeless. He knew that he desired Tamar as he had never desired anyone in his life before; and he knew that she was forbidden to him. Forbidden by the law, by his father, by his brothers, by his duty to cherish and protect her. These contradictory facts maintained a perfect equipoise in his mind, as if he had indeed been split in two; there was no communication, no connection, between them. It was only later that they came together in knowledge of one another and interpenetrated with one another, so that he could accuse himself of loving her because she was forbidden to him; or could accuse God, society, and his father of forbidding her to him because he had been bound to love her. (Yes, I assure the psychoanalytically-minded among you that these rudimentary insights were vouchsafed very early and quite spontaneously to our interesting case, A.) By then he was deep in his labyrinth, isolated in the rooms of the house his father had given him. During that time he didn't see anyone apart from his servants, until the night he sent for me. As for Tamar, he claimed he had left the room that evening without looking at her again. He did not need to; he could not bear to.

4

Ladies and gentlemen, I have a confession to make. I am in some doubt about how to proceed with the next part of my story. You know, as I do, that Amnon is not going to be able to resist his desire for his sister Tamar, he is not going to rise above it, he is not going to be restrained either by pity for her or by dread of the consequences of pursuing her. But with that knowledge common to us both, how can I make real to you, or interesting to you (it amounts to the same thing) the torments of indecision Amnon went through before he finally succumbed to what thus became his fate. His prayers, his insomnia, his bouts of drunkenness, his vows of chastity, his threats to commit suicide, his hastily conceived and hastily abandoned plans to leave the country – what nonsense all these will seem to you, what a waste of time, when you see them (as you must) as a tedious preface to a foregone conclusion. How can you possibly sympathise with the agony of his vacillation when you have the certainty of knowing what he actually did – and must do again each time the story is told, for as long as it continues to be told?

Very well then, you may say, let's just accept that he went through such a period, and get on with what followed it. But the problem is not quite so simple. As far as Amnon is concerned, the torment he suffered before he acted is important not merely because it happened, so to speak, and thus is entitled to its place in the story, but because of the consequences it had. If you do not understand how much Amnon had to overcome within himself, how keen was his own sense of the enormity of the crime he wanted to commit, then I am afraid you will also be unable to understand his subsequent actions, which, wild and brutal though they may have been, yet followed their own logic of hope and despair.

That's one point. The second weighs with me a little more, perhaps. It isn't just for Amnon's sake that I dwell on the difficulty he had in making up his mind to act as he did. No, it's for the sake of the figure that I, Yonadab, am to cut in this story. Allow me my measure of vanity, too, my desire to appear to have influenced the course of events. Crucially.

I urged Amnon to commit the crime, I encouraged him to go after Tamar, I teased him for being cowardly and split-minded, I told him of the special affection for him that I pretended I had seen in Tamar's eyes, I reminded him of the freedom he had by virtue of his position as the king's eldest son. Yet what status will I have in your eyes as meddler, middleman, pander, if you simply take it for granted that Amnon was bound to have done what he did anyway: if you do not realise, that is to say, just how evenly balanced were the impulses inside him? (Though that delicate image of a balance hardly indicates the crazed lurchings of his temperament and will.) If you are to have any respect for me, any feeling that I am more than a mere narrator but an active participant in the story, then it is essential that you should see Amnon poised between two equally possible courses of action, and me at his elbow guiding and advising him to take the one he eventually took. Had I behaved differently, I do believe he might indeed have left the country, or Jerusalem at least, or consoled himself with other women, or transformed his desire for Tamar into a passion of another kind – religious, perhaps, or warlike. I worked hard on him, I can tell you; and I know, however it might seem to you who have the benefit of hindsight, that I wasn't wasting my breath.

All right, you want to know why I did what I did? Why else, except for the reason I have just given! To feel that I counted for something in the court; that my words had consequences; that my presence had made a difference to events. That's why. A modest ambition, in the circumstances.

Also, I will tell you that I had a certain grudge against Tamar, as you may already have suspected from my description of her. Say it was a grudge I had against all David's children, for having so many advantages over me. But there was more to it than that in Tamar's case. There was a quality of inattention about her – at least as far as I was concerned – that I found very difficult indeed to forgive. Especially as my intolerable father, in one of his more ambitious moods, had suggested to his equally intolerable brother that I might be a suitable *parti* for the girl. The king had rejected me out of hand, and I admit I have no real reason to suppose that Tamar had ever got to hear about it. But I still found her lack of curiosity about me insulting to a degree. Did she imagine that I was too low, too insignificant, to be worthy of focussing those dark eyes of hers upon? In that case, she was wrong. But only on condition, you understand, that I could have saved her, and instead helped to damage her, ruin her, break her life apart.

I see that I can, in fact, do no more than state my problem: I cannot resolve it. Amnon's torment of indecision is something that he simply has to endure, without witnesses. He endures it. I whisper in his ear what I must, and what only Amnon will ever hear. He comes to his decision. Choice once made, the illusion of choice ceases to exist; it is as though it has never been. The period he has just gone through appears absurd and craven to us both. And tedious too. Just as it would be to you if I were to go through it stage by stage, word by word, scene by scene. Now the rest can follow. Time to begin again what we began then.

So it was, or is, that Amnon approaches and tells me quietly, his face taut yet puckered, two prim, disgusted lines running down either side of his jaw, as with the jaw of a puppet, 'I've made up my mind'.

The quietness of his voice and the stiffness of his carriage are also new. I have seen him look like this only once before: when we were boys, when we had been sent to get the smell of battle in one of his father's wars, and Amnon had made up his mind to go into the front line, no matter what the officer who had been put in charge of us should do or say. His face – boyish and unmarked then – and his body had been turned, as they are now, towards a self-chosen, never-to-be-averted fate. That time all had turned out well. I doubt if it will do so again.

I don't pretend that I need to ask him which way his decision has gone. 'Of course. I always knew you would.'

'You lie.' I don't respond, so he says it again. 'You lie, you bastard.' He still hasn't raised his voice, yet he manages to compress into it the hatred he suddenly feels towards me. For being his ally; for encouraging him to follow the course he has taken; even for having known at once what he was talking about. Days have passed since we last saw each other, and then we hadn't spoken about Tamar; our present meeting has taken place by chance, in the street, in broad daylight. Preoccupied with my own affairs, my eyes cast downwards to avoid the glare of the

45

sun, I hadn't noticed Amnon until he had called my name out; and then he had spoken without any preamble or preliminary. Now he stands in front of me, stalwart, swarthy, haggard, braced by his own will, and calls me a liar, a bastard, a cheat, and many other unpleasant things. His thick lips move busily, and I watch them without really listening to the words they are producing. I think of those lips pressed flat upon Tamar's pale face. Yes! Yes, it is right that Amnon should be ugly, that when you look at him you should think of bulls, idols, archaic statuary, misshapen trees, apes from Africa. He is fitted for his role, fated for it, as I am, I suppose (but can never really believe), for mine. Which includes his abuse, the hot sunlight pouring down upon us both, these people passing by, that barefoot, doubled-up porter staggering along under a great, lolling load of offal in a bag, which is tied to him by a single band of leather around his forehead. And those flies following him, in a frenziedly spinning, singing halo.

Then, with barely a pause between abuse and request for assistance, and with hardly a change of tone, Amnon says, 'I need your help.'

'Why?'

He swears at me again, but less energetically than before, and for a shorter time. Then there comes the same request. 'You must help me.' It is plainly inconceivable to him that I shouldn't do so. 'We must talk about it. Not now, but soon. As soon as possible.'

In my opinion, he is wrong. For my part, there's no need for haste. Between this moment and the moment of consummation there are thousands that he still has to endure; but I have no doubt that he will go through them to the end. Henceforth any delays or diversions will only harden his resolve, inflame him all the more, make more vivid his fantasies. Accordingly, I can let him stew in his own juice; the juice will be so much the ranker as a result.

So I pretend to be quite as eager as he is to meet as soon as possible, to discuss the matter further, to formulate the plans he is obviously expecting me to think up. (Amnon is enough of a realist, I see, to know that I am cleverer than he is.) It is imperative that we should meet, yes, I agree, I do understand that. But alas, I tell him, it isn't possible. As it happens, I declare untruthfully, but with great regret, I am on the very point of leaving Jerusalem for several days. On official business. Something my father has asked me to do. No, it can't be put off. I can't let my father down. It's out of the question. Not even to help Amnon at such a moment of crisis. But, I point out to him – untruthfully again, and knowing that he will disagree with me violently – now that he has come to his decision, the worst is over; now he can afford to relax, to take things easy. Now he is in a position to enjoy the delights of anticipation. I am even bold enough to hint that these delights may be more intense than those of achievement. This is the first truth I have uttered for a few minutes, but it is one which no keen anticipator could ever accept: if he did, he would cease to be one and would become instead someone like myself.

Predictably, I succeed only in angering Amnon. But he doesn't swear at me now. He asks me if we can't meet that night; if I can't come to his house right away; if we can't just stay where we are and talk the matter over in the street. No, none of these is possible either. I simply haven't the time. Moreover, I tell him, we must be circumspect from now on; we mustn't draw attention to ourselves, as we are doing by standing in the middle of the street and talking together like a couple of merchants. People are looking at us; they are not used to seeing men

47

dressed in court robes in such an attitude. They will think that something is amiss unless we leave each other now in a calm, superior manner.

'Let them look!' Amnon shouts. His voice is suddenly triumphant, that of a man who has found himself at last. 'I'll give them something to stare at, you wait and see!'

Poor devil. He will, indeed. Already he sees in their whispers and sidelong glances – what? His name on their children's lips, his picture in museums, books written about him, flowers of the field named after him. A place for him in the hearts of them all; and a place in his heart for all of them, his life being a summation and justification of their unknown, nameless existences. Poor devil? More keenly than ever before, hearing that cry from his throat, seeing his rapt face, his lips curved in an inanely exalted smile, I envy him. To have a destiny is nothing: each of us has a destiny, no matter how niggardly or miserable it may be. But to believe in it, even fleetingly, to accept it as the only one possible for you: that is something else again. Amnon is in that state, not I; I never will be.

All the more reason to let him stew in his own juice, then.

'I must be going. I'll come to see you immediately I get back into town.'

'Not a moment later.'

He turns to go. But some instinct of prudence or pride forces him to say, with a feeble attempt at nonchalance, 'You might be too late. By then I might have nothing to say to you.'

That is a risk I must run. I don't believe it to be a great one. Not if I know Amnon. I smile and answer, 'For your sake I hope it may be so.'

We part, Amnon going up towards the palace, I away from it. But I have taken only a few paces when I hear

Amnon's footsteps behind me. He halts me again, putting his hand on my shoulder.

'You see,' he says, in a tone that is now one of laboured, fanatical reasonableness, as of a man clinging to his faith in rational procedures and explanations, in the teeth of all temptations to abandon them, 'You see, I have to break the law in order to show that I'm really free to obey it. You understand what I mean? If I obey it just because I'm too scared to do anything else, then what is my obedience worth? But afterwards . . . if I obey it . . . then it will be because the law really has meaning for me, because I understand it, because I'm a man who's set himself free to do the other thing and yet chooses not to. Do you see what I mean?'

His essay in logic is concluded. I want to cry 'Bravo!' To think that Amnon could work through such a piece of jesuitical casuistry all on his own! Amnon, whom no one in the world has ever accused of being particularly strong in the top storey. Filth and impiety for the sake of a freer, more godlike piety (in a little while, later, in the end, after he's had his sport) – what could be better? Talk about eating your cake and having it! It just goes to show what really passionate desire can do to exercise the mind.

'Yes,' I say. 'I do see what you mean, Amnon. I won't forget what you've just said.'

This time he leaves me without looking or coming back. I go on my way. I have to leave Jerusalem for a few days, which I hadn't planned to do, and is a little inconvenient at such short notice. Never mind. I have something to look forward to when I get back.

Keeping out of Amnon's way for a few days, I went to the country, to one of my father's properties, a farm that eventually passed into my possession. You may go there today and have a look at it, if you like: take the road that winds eastwards out of Bethlehem, going downhill, and then curving south between the hills. You won't have far to go. The further you travel along the road, the barer the countryside becomes; with every mile that passes there are fewer terraces and ploughed fields, fewer groves of olive trees – their trunks clamped into grotesquely arthritic postures, their silver leaves above improbably delicate and pure. The flat roofs of the villagers' huts ascend the slopes against which they are built like broken flights of steps, leading nowhere, always abandoning half-way their attempts to reach the summits that tower above them. On every hill great circular bands of limestone, each narrower in circumference than the one beneath it, are piled upon one another with a regularity that is abstract, almost dream-like, in its effect; and the lowest of these bands wind across the valleys in wide loops that join hill to hill, and so make them all seem part of a pattern the eye can perceive but cannot contain. There, amid such scenery, you come to the farm I owned, you come to the village from which our house stood a little apart, with its orchards and grazing fields behind it. You are on the very crest of the country, its last inhabited ridge, where the rain clouds that come in from the sea, during their season, die away into wisps of vapour, so that distances of barely more than a few hundreds of yards, east or west, can mean the difference between absolute drought and meagre growth. Westwards, hills like those you have travelled through go back to Hebron. But if you climb the slope immediately to the east of where our house stood, and surmount it, you will see the wilderness at your feet. Behind you the landscape is composed of features to which you can give names, as I have done: you call them hills, valleys, *wadis*, terraces, limestone bands, villages, peaks. For what is in front of you, there are no names.

Oh yes, there is one. A dull, flat, acidic burn, a leaden light: the Dead Sea. The rest is without form or shape, there is nothing for your gaze to rest on, nothing that compels it to go from one point to any other, nothing it returns to with any sense of renewal or reward. The lifts and falls of the earth do not make up hills and valleys, they do not go back in folds, but are merely fissured humps, random lumps and mounds of matter, all utterly bare, all of an illusory, corrupt softness of appearance, as if the stuff of which they are made could be broken off by the hand into pliable masses. Even the colours out there are not real colours, but, changing in the light, seem always to be in a process of becoming something other than they are, disintegrating into shades of yellow, red, mauve, white, dirtier yet than those you see. Not a road, not a hut, not even a tree. But the imagination involuntarily seizes upon vague patches of colour, on scattered boulders, on the meetings of one crevice with others, and makes of these phantom villages or pathways; then the illusion goes and you realise that you have merely tried once again to make the unknowable conform to something you already know. To your left and right it stretches away, distance opening upon distance equally at every point. In the east your horizon remains a single jagged line, the cliffs of Moab, a gulf, a maw, forever wedged wide open in its impossible attempt to swallow the sky.

There it is: the wilderness on my doorstep. It never changes; that is the nature of a wilderness. It never goes out of date. It does not lend itself to any of our plans or purposes. It does not care whether we look over it or not. It is very boring. Many roads run to its edge.

Since no one else is likely to say it, I have to do so myself: there was a touch of genius in the plan I worked out for Amnon during the few days I spent unexpectedly in the country. My plan for bringing him together with Tamar could be grandly called a series of interlocking ironies; but for all its inward complexity, it had the merit as well of being simple and to the point. In retrospect and anticipation, I don't know which aspect of the plan gives me more satisfaction, its simplicity or its complexity. Both, at any rate, contributed equally to its success.

I am boasting, yes. But consider the difficulties I had to overcome in bringing the two of them together; in bringing them together alone; in bringing them together for a time long enough for Amnon to declare his love to her and then to demonstrate it in whatever way he chose. (Not that I had any doubt, after listening to him, which way he would choose.) The difficulties in the way of such a meeting don't seem so great to you? Oh dear, it seems that we are faced here with what the anthropologists call a culture-gap, which can be crossed only by a certain stretching of the imagination on your side, a certain amount of deliberate explication on mine.

I will put the matter as baldly as I can, to begin with. Tamar lived in a harem. That is what the women's quarters of David's palace must be called. Now do you begin to get an idea of my difficulties? But I beg you not to be carried away by your memories of Hollywood movies, say, or of booklets of pornographic pictures acquired on the Charing Cross Road. Put out of your mind those portraits of languid houris lying about in attitudes suggestive of inner heats; forget those eunuchs in baggy silken pants brandishing scimitars outside mysterious, ogee-arched doorways. It wasn't like that. The women's quarters of David's palace were quiet, domestic, respectable. Indeed, almost suburban. After all, your suburbs, too, are pretty much inhabited by women and children only during the daylight hours. Confined to their areas by day and night, David's women chattered, promenaded, ate, looked after their children, quarrelled, weaved cloth, sewed, and generally passed their time as best they could. On high festivals they emerged to watch the sacrifices and parades from specially erected pavilions; when a visitor of great importance arrived they crowded their roof-terraces to see what they could of his reception. Of course, many distinctions were observed among them. Even among the king's official wives there were some who had larger apartments, more clothes, more jewels, and more servants than others; his concubines were invariably less generously treated, and any one among them who fell out of favour was likely to find herself relegated to being the servant of another.

That was the world in which Tamar had grown up: a cross, you might say, between a brothel with a single patron, an unusually secluded girls' school or hospital for women, and a family home. Confusing, doubtless. But not so much more, perhaps, than your suburbs: merely different. Incidentally, the seclusion of the harem was maintained less by porters and patrolling guards than by the sheer numbers of women who lived in it. They were a far more effective watch upon one another than whole squads of scimitar-brandishing, baggy-pantalooned eunuchs ever could be. If your suburban adulterers often find themselves plagued by their neighbours, I don't need to elaborate on how difficult it was for anything clandestine to take place in that part of the palace, with all its half-curtained doorways, its open courtyards and rooftops, its busy corridors. Even in the smallest hours of the night the place was likely to be astir with women who couldn't sleep, or who had got up to go to the lavatory, or who were walking their crying children about.

Still, even given all these circumstances, my difficulties might have been less than they were if Tamar had lived in the harem as one of David's wives or mistresses, rather than as his virgin daughter. A married woman, even one married to a king, always has reasons for leaving her husband for a few days. Her mother is sick, her sister is having a baby, her brother is trying to swindle her out of her estate and her presence is needed at home. These are just a few suggestions or excuses; the married women among you have, I'm sure, used others; and I dare say so had David's wives, who from time to time did leave the palace on their own affairs, lumbering off in closely escorted caravans along the stony roads that wound down, east and west, north and south, from our mountain city. But the case was different with the girls in the harem, David's daughters. They were captives entirely. No claims from outside the palace were ever made on them; there was nothing that could be offered to them from any quarter of the kingdom that David himself did not provide.

And if so much was true of any virgin daughter of the king, remember what Tamar, and Tamar alone, was to David. The walls that surrounded her can be thought of as nothing more or less than a physical representation of his love and care; and you may be certain that he kept them in the best possible order. She had her own set of rooms, her own teachers and servants, who were all frequently questioned about her welfare; David himself made a point of seeing her whenever he could, even if it was just for a few minutes in the day. Of all that he valued, she was the most greatly valued; of all he protected, as king and father, she was the most protected.

Which is why, thinking about what had to be accomplished, I eventually decided, much to my own surprise, that it was David himself who had to make the opening for Amnon in the walls that surrounded her: no one else could do it. She had to come to Amnon not behind the king's back, not in despite of the king, still less in rebellion against him, but with his approval; indeed, at his command. There was no other way it could be done. David must willingly turn the key that only David held. Amnon's ideas of grabbing at her in corridors, of trying to sneak unobserved into her apartments, of passing messages to her through servants, of somehow abducting her from the palace and riding hell-for-leather with her, in high romantic fashion, into the deserts of Moab or Edom – all these schemes, which sure enough Amnon was to gabble out to me when I returned to the city, were a waste of time, so many dead-ends. They wouldn't work. Whereas once David's co-operation had been secured, Amnon would surely have the time and the opportunity he sought.

Obvious enough, it now seems. But to arrive at it required that everything both Amnon and I had at first imagined about his next move should be turned on its head. Only then did it seem obvious, as our best, most unexpected ideas often do.

But why, you will ask, as I asked myself, should the king agree to releasing Tamar, however temporarily, from her confinement? What could persuade him to do so? And here the answer I eventually arrived at was again the obvious, utterly unexpected one. The truth, that's all! Not the whole truth, indeed; but the truth nevertheless. Amnon didn't have to dissimulate; I wasn't going to ask him to tell any elaborate lies. All he had to do was to let his father know that he had fallen ill – which was assuredly the truth: he was sick, diseased, a case: anyone could see it – and then, once he had succeeded in arousing his father's compassion and anxiety, he had to ask for Tamar to be sent to him, because he felt sure that only she could cure his illness. And what, I ask you, could be truer than that?

But the final, and in my view the most delicious irony was that the king would think his request a reasonable one, and would be likely to release Tamar and send her to her undoing, precisely for the reasons that made him at all other times guard her so closely. Nothing would seem more natural to him than that the presence of his adored Tamar should be asked for by Amnon. He liked to believe that her purity and beauty, the moral effect of her whole being, had the power to make the wrong right, the bad good, the ill well; he himself sought out her company in his spells of despondency and unease. Then how could he be surprised that her brother should do the same when he was suffering, perhaps was in real danger, from a malady neither he nor his doctors could explain?

Hindsight tempts one to pretend to foresight. Everything that follows is indeed the result of my plan; but I would be lying if I stage-managed events in such a way as to make you think that I anticipated what actually happened. The truth is I made no further plans, I did not really define my expectations. But I suppose I could sum them up easily enough. Mischief. Excitement. Trouble. The pleasure of instigating and observing it all and the pleasure, if possible, of getting away with it too.

As you will see, I was not to be disappointed. Amnon, Tamar and David obliged me equally; and so did Absalom, when his turn came.

For my own safety I relied initially on Amnon's pride,

I might add, not his loyalty or charity. What could he say? How much blame would he ever be able to put effectively on me? To what end? 'Please sir, Yonadab suggested I should fall in love with my sister, so I did it.' That wouldn't sound very princely or heroic. It wouldn't be true either; but that's by the way. 'Please sir, I fell in love with my sister, so I asked Yonadab, you see, what I should do next, and he said I should pretend to be sick and ask Tamar to be sent to me – which is what I did, so everything that's happened is really his fault.' Well, that story would be a little truer than the first; but again, how shaming, how diminishing, how comic really, is the mention of my name; how helpless a fool it makes him appear to be. How different the effect of such a confession would be from, 'Yes, I love my sister Tamar, and would break any law, defy any power, overcome any difficulty, to be near her'. Or, 'You can try to kill me, you can destroy my body; but it is too late, for what I've taken from Tamar has made me immortal, beyond your touch'. Or even, 'I can only pray that you, my father, and you, my dear sister Tamar, and you, my brothers, will wipe the evil I've done from your memories as completely as I now wipe out my life with this single blow – !'

Fine, dramatic speeches, all of them, worthy to be remembered by young lovers and rebels for ages ahead. Or so I was sure I could persuade Amnon to feel, even if I'd had to choose one of them for him and rehearse it with him beforehand. Of course, such speeches presuppose the very worst that could happen to Amnon. But there were other possibilities, plenty of them. A clandestine affair that no one but the two of them (and myself) would ever know about. No consequences at all: one huddled, desperate encounter, and a lifetime of black secrecy (to which I would be privy) thereafter. A runaway match. A confession to David, a great row, and a swift alteration of the law by David, in order to make an honest woman out of Tamar; followed no doubt by handfuls of would-be Nathans and has-been Samuels coming to the court to prophesy woe and doom. . . .

I must be boring you with these speculations about events that never took place. They have a certain intricate attraction for me, somehow, existing as they do only in a time that is never of time. Not even of the simulacrum of time in which you and I have managed to meet.

5

The power of the truth! Imagine the king and Amnon together in Amnon's bedroom, their arms around one another's necks, tears in their eyes, and pleas for forgiveness falling from their lips. They are closer to one another than they have ever been before. Why? Because Amnon, having gasped out that the illness he is suffering from is going to kill him (and which of us can now say that he is wrong?), has gone on to tell the king that he is a bad son, that the king doesn't know how evil he is, how rotten, how unfit to touch the king's hand. (And which of us would like to argue the issue with him?)

Amnon's spirit, in short, is shattered by the remorse he feels over the action he has yet to commit; and the effect of his self-abasement on the king is overwhelming. David confesses that he hasn't shown enough love for Amnon and enough appreciation of his wonderful qualities; he hasn't listened carefully enough to him; he hasn't been as good a father as he should have been. But if only Amnon will rally and recover, then there will be a new love and respect between them and they will never look back on the failures of the past.

An affecting scene. The hairs of Amnon's beard start out of his skin with a stiff, swooping curve, as if about to take off from his face altogether; his eyes move about in starts, jumps, hops, like a pair of toads. He strokes his father's hand and kisses it, while the king turns his head away and buries it in the crook of his free arm. It would all be enough to make me gush forth with tears, too, if only the truths that are at last being blubbed and stammered into the air of the bedroom were not making even murkier the treachery at their heart. For you need have no fear: lying there, Amnon is not undergoing a spiritual reformation that will bring him back like the hero of a serial from the edge of the dreadful abyss into which he is about to plunge, etcetera. Far from it. In Amnon's bulging, in-flamed eyes I can see a frank astonishment and pleasure alongside the remorse he is feeling. He is amazed at his unprecedented closeness to his father; at the tenderness that has so suddenly taken the place of the surliness and irony that always spoiled their relationship before. If he and his father have reached this state merely in anticipation of the ruin of the creature his father loves best in the world, imagine what might yet pass between them after it has happened!

No, lying on his bed with his arms around his father's shoulders, Amnon is far from giving up his scheme. Instead, between groans and shivers of the most racked, wholehearted kind, he is probably wondering why he didn't think of it before.

What if David is not a vain, cunning and self-deceiving old man, as I see him; but a true figure or pattern of royalty, worthy to be God's chosen and anointed one, his surrogate on earth and mankind's great spokesman in the courts of heaven? That is how David often thinks of himself, I know: what if David is right? What if Amnon is not an impulsive, violent, thick-headed fellow, but the very type of the flawed hero of a classical tragedy; the man with a single weakness of will or aberration of desire that inevitably brings about his moral degeneration and death? And what if Tamar and Absalom, too, whom you hardly know as yet, are not only wrong-headed and ill-fated, but heroic and brilliant as well? Yes, what if all the people I have spoken of are to be remembered for their passionate fullness of life; and not as I do, chiefly, for their confusion and absurdity?

I suspect that you have long been asking such questions of yourselves. Fair enough. My answer to them is that I was a Kantian (of a kind) long before I had ever heard of Kant. That is, I've always felt that one can come no closer to 'the truth' about the world than one's given faculties of mind and modes of perception permit. If I see meagreness where others see riches; vanity where others see prowess; meaninglessness where others see divine purpose; theatricality and role-playing where others see fate and passion; farce where others see tragedy – then that is just my bad luck, if you like, and there is no need for you to glower reproachfully at me, as though I have wilfully chosen to let the side down. Yonadab can live only in Yonadab's world.

But I'm not that much of a Philistine – in the modern sense of the word, I mean; I'm not referring to our ancient tribal enemies – I'm not that much of a Philistine as not to wonder, often, what it must be like to be someone other than myself, and to view the world through a set of pre-possessions entirely different from my own. For example, if we are to go back to the scene in Amnon's bedroom which I interrupted a moment ago, I am quite prepared to wonder how it must feel to be David, as he gently disengages himself from Amnon's embrace, and then sinks slowly to the floor, prostrating himself in prayer for the well-being of his son.

I follow his example immediately, of course, and so do the two equerries who have come as escort to him on this visit. It would obviously not do for us to remain upright when the king is on the floor. Once we are down, it is understood that we are also deep in prayer. However, obsessed with the idea of trying to penetrate his consciousness, I am keeping my eyes on the king.

The angle from which I view him is a curious one, and having covered my face with my hands, I have to peer at him through a heavy grille of my own fingers. Flat expanses of multi-coloured rugs stretch away from me like a prospect of flowers; at the far end the drapes from Amnon's bed hang down like a wall. The huddled shape of the king is at its foot. I can only see his head and shoulders, and they convey little to me. They could be those of a sleeping peasant, not of a priest-king in prayer; allowing for the fine linen he is wearing, that is. When he rises again to his feet it is even more difficult for me to see him, because I don't dare get up until I am quite sure he would wish me to. But I can roll over a little to one side, to try and make out what he's up to. Through the gaps between my fingers I see him throw back his head and raise his arms so that his wide sleeves fall back over his sinewy elbows. He remains like that, his arms pointing upwards prophetically, his beard tilted up, his eyes closed. There is a faint tremor to his hands.

Now: to leap inside his head. Can it be done? I close my eyes. I try to imagine myself standing as David does, arms upraised, an appeal to God streaming out of me, starting forth like a spiritual force from my fingertips and the very point of my beard. Does the force travel from me in psychic waves, quanta, emanations? Can it be translated into words? How do I know that it is travelling in the right direction? All right, let me say that I simply know it to be going in the right direction, that I do not care what form it takes, that if I could describe or categorise it in any way it would cease to be what it is. It goes, goes, goes, goes, streaming upwards, derived from above and beneath my personal preoccupations: Amnon's health, my anxiety about him, my guilt towards him, the dark memories which such guilts and anxieties arouse in me, my hopes that the future might take one course rather than others. All of these are known to me; but I am seeking to express and discharge that in myself which I do not know, and never will know, the very self of self, whole and undistracted, summoned up and directed to a single end. And what is the end? Only that that last self should be known by what is not-me, outside me, ever beyond me: that I should become the unknowing knower, known by the unknown. Then the force that streams out of me is not lost but returns with a power greater than before, it is what knocks in my heart, flows with my blood, I have become its vessel and instrument. I have ceased to be myself, yet I shall never be more myself than I am now. My prayer hasn't been answered, how could it be, it hasn't even been formulated yet, but my presence, my need, my being, has been acknowledged.

The moment accomplished, it falls out of time; I cannot live in it or with it. It leaves me, I must leave it, I must return to my time and my known self, the personal, demanding self of guilt and duty. But I do not return as I went. Now I can speak, now I can find words suitable to a

62

king in his capital city, a father standing alongside his son, an old man in a sickroom. I can call on the source of all power and all time for the welfare and safety of whatever is mine; I can ask for such measure of peace and repose as a man can hope to have.

So David finishes his prayer. He is a little flushed from the exertion he has just been through, but his expression is serene. His faith has been restored and refreshed. He believes that his interests may indeed have become, for that lost, immeasurable moment, identical with those of the universe: nothing less.

And I? Yonadab on the floor, breathing in the dust of the rugs? Can I get up now? It seems safe to do so. Thank you. The two officers rise as well, with every manifestation of awe and humility. I smooth down my robes. I ask myself, in my own character once more, what David's powers and prayers are worth if he still has no idea of why his son is prostrated, and what the consequences of that prostration are likely to be. The safety of his house! The welfare of his son! Would it have been asking too much of that unknown Lord of Lords of his to drop him the tiniest hint about what is going on? Apparently so.

Amnon, too, is more relaxed, I see. The performance has not made him even more anguished in his guilt than before, but has helped to calm him, encouraging him to feel, it seems, that he too has access to supernatural resources. His eyes no longer jump about; his voice is no longer choked with dread and hysteria. He asks the king if he may have a word with him alone. The king agrees without demur. We go out of the room, the two officers and I. Not for the first time it strikes me how much of the authority of the king springs from his readiness to permit others to witness what ordinary men would try to keep most jealously private. The presence of others at such times, if he chooses to have them there, is necessary to him precisely so that they may be ignored.

We do not have long to wait. When the king comes out his manner is a shade less assured. But I cannot read from it his mood or state of mind. Suspicion? Puzzlement? Irritation? It could be any of these. I catch a single, sharp glance in my direction, as if he wonders just what my relationship to Amnon is. It is disconcerting to be the object of such a flicker of attention, when it comes from a man who has the power of life and death over you. For some reason – for an obvious reason – I remind myself, as I follow the king out of the house, that he has never indulged himself in the pastime of torturing those who have fallen out of his favour. Killing them, or tipping a wink so discreet that only the murderous sons of Zeruiah, Joab and Abishai, for whom it is intended, ever see it – that is his style. But (allowing for one regrettable lapse after the capture of Rabbat-Ammon) he has never gone in for lingering cruelties; it is just one among the sophistications which, to his credit, he has declined to learn from our predecessors in Canaan and our neighbours to the north. It isn't for my own sake only that I find these reflections comforting, while I walk dutifully behind him; I have no wish to see Amnon under the rake.

In the lane outside the house there wait the king's litter, his torchbearers, the horses of the equerries, and a platoon of soldiers, some of whom are holding back the inevitable crowd of gapers and idlers. The people in the front rank of the crowd kneel when the king appears, and from them all a cry of greeting goes up, which the king acknowledges with a wave of his hand, hardly bothering to look in their direction. Shadows flap and dance against the walls, expanding and contracting with the rising and falling of the flames of the torches. The king is assisted into his covered litter. The soldiers begin to clear a way through the throng. The king's cheek gleams red in a sudden gust of flame, through the half-open curtain of the litter; his beard is of silver, his eyelids wearily lowered. He looks like a statue, an artefact, a painted monarch. He has not paid any attention to me since first coming out of Amnon's room.

I ask him if he wishes me to return to the palace with him.

'There's no need.'

I am dismissed. The porters stoop, the curtains jerk and are closed. The king has concluded his visit to his ailing son. The company makes its way up the cobbled lane to the palace, whose outer walls are no more than several hundred yards away. I go back into Amnon's house.

The night passed. I spent it with Amnon. By the time I left him in the morning, he had already bathed, changed his bedclothes, and combed his beard and hair, in anticipation of the visit which the king had promised his sister would be making to him that evening. He was excited beyond measure; almost stupefied with impatience. But I was overcome with an emotion that surprised me disagreeably. It was remorse.

It seemed that I resembled Amnon more than I had supposed: in itself a disagreeable discovery. He also had been afflicted with an anticipatory remorse: I had found it rather comic at the time. Now it was my turn. The whole day – a late summer's day like any other, dry, dusty, the sky alternating in glares of white and yellow until it all became darker and more lurid towards sunset – I felt a wretched glumness that shifted about within me, as it were, but never lessened or left me. My mood was like one of those that afflict you (that afflicted me at any rate) in adolescence, in which everything you see appears to be both the occasion for the spirit's sadness and an expression of it. Even the stones in the ground, if you know what I mean.

I ramble. But so did my thoughts. Only, at their core, never forgotten, was a point of grief, a precise sorrow. What had I done! Why had I done it? What malevolence within me had made it possible?

Yet nothing had happened. There was still time for me to rush over to the king and confess all. Of course, I did not do so. That was how much my remorse was worth: which merely made it all the more intolerable. I mooned over the work I was supposed to be doing; I went from time to time to the window of my office and looked out in the direction of Amnon's house; I looked in the direction of the women's quarters of the palace, where Tamar, too, was perhaps excitedly and innocently preparing herself for her evening's expedition. She must have been very flattered when she had heard from the king how much Amnon needed her. How she would relish the role she was being asked to play; how well it would fit in with her notion of her own importance! Another irony, that; but it gave me no pleasure to think of it. I went back to my desk and stared at the rolls and tallies accumulated on it, shuffled them about in what I assure you was already the traditional fashion, swore absently at my scribe, and returned to the window.

I was working, by the way, in the equivalent of your Ministry of Public Works; not the most inspiriting of jobs under the best of circumstances. Ministry of Forced Labour you could call it: we had the responsibility of administering the *corvée* which was exacted from the general population, Israelites and others alike. (Though on the whole we bore more heavily on the others than on the Israelites). It was a much-detested institution, you won't be surprised to hear. So much so, that the man I shared my office with, Adoram by name – a hardworking, unimaginative careerist, whose successive promotions kept pace with the department's growth in national importance – was eventually to be stoned to death when an enraged mob recognised him during the troubles that beset the kingdom in the days of David's grandson. The fitting end to a devoted career. A prevision of his fate might have cheered me up that afternoon, when I looked across from my desk to the head bent so studiously over his; but unfortunately none was granted to me.

I left the office early and returned to Amnon's house. I don't know what he'd been doing during my absence – bathing and pomading himself a few more times, doubtless. Anyway, he was shiningly clean, offensively scented, combed like a horse before a big parade. The whole place was swept and aired, and there were new cloths on the tables and new hangings on the walls. Amnon was still excited and talkative, but offhand now as well. Striding and wheeling to and fro, exactly like an overfed stallion, he talked a great deal about his 'illness' as if it had been a real illness of which I knew very little, if you please. He spoke with a kind of hypochondriacal pluck about how much he was looking forward to being 'well' again, how much he envied people who never had to worry about their health, how difficult it was to convey to someone like myself the anxieties and sick fancies a man could become subject to when he was 'cooped up' for weeks on end. I could hardly believe my ears. Of Tamar he said not a word. When I mentioned her name, he stopped in mid-prance, stared at me with an air of surprise and affrontment, and then went on with what he'd been talking about before.

It was more than I could stand. Especially after the day of useless apprehension and regret I had been through. So it had become a piece of tactlessness on my part to mention Tamar's name? Was that the stage we'd reached? Not bloody likely. And I told him so, too.

The result was that we had a fierce row. At first he still tried to take a high line with me, looking haughty and indifferent, not deigning to answer my jeers and reminders of all I knew and all I had done for him. But it didn't take long to break him down. He was soon yelling at me, his face contorted, his fists clenched; he advanced on me, thrust his face a few inches from mine, and told me that he was going to kill me, that he'd had enough of my interference in his affairs, that he knew I'd always been plotting to ruin him. But he'd ruin me, he'd smash me. And so on.

Until our anger left us both, almost as suddenly as it had come. It was followed by silence, embarrassment, unease about the threats we had just uttered, reluctance on the part of either of us to apologise to the other. I wished I were somewhere else, but found that I could not believe in the possibility of leaving. Not by any means. Not even if Amnon ordered me to, or called on his servants to throw me out. Only then, indeed, did I realise that my desire to be in his house, to stay until Tamar arrived and as long as I could thereafter, was not so much a desire as a compulsion, an imperative that I could not disobey. My own growing sense of choicelessness in the matter had been a part, I now understood, of the depression I had been feeling all day. To be present, to peep, to gloat, perhaps to let Tamar know just how much I knew – all these, which I had previously thought of as my rewards for the work I had done, now appeared to me in the dreary aspect of so many duties which I had to carry out, irrespective of my inclinations. The fact that those duties had not long before actually been my inclinations could only make them so much the more distasteful to me now.

I suppose some of you will conclude that I tell you this in order to make you think better of me. You are wrong. I think rather the worse of myself, if anything, because of my inability to take pleasure in my achievement. What a typical trick it was for my psyche to play upon itself! Anyhow, I'm sure you will all understand that I wasn't keen on trying to explain to Amnon the inner complexities of my attitude. Even if he'd been able to understand me, which I doubted, he would probably not have believed me. So what to do?

Nothing.

The silence prolonged itself. Finally Amnon stepped back a few paces, looking warily at me; then, as if it were safe to do so only when he was some distance from me, he turned and went through the arched doorway that led into an inner room, and from there through a little ante-chamber into his bedroom. I heard him throw himself down on his bed. Presumably he had suffered a sudden relapse in the course of that famous illness of his. I stood where I was for some time, before going to sit on a stool. Through a high, unshuttered window I watched the slow darkening of a bruise-coloured square of light, which was all I could see of the sky. Then I had an idea. I walked through to the entrance of Amnon's bedroom. He was lying on his back, with a hand over his eyes.

'You know that you really want me to be here when she comes,' I said. 'So why pretend otherwise?'

Amnon answered me without lifting his hand from his face. 'I don't care what you do.'

It was a good enough answer for me; it said as much as I could have expected. I went back to my stool in the living-room. Later Amnon joined me. We even managed to make a little conversation with one another, while we waited.

6

I hope you appreciate the trouble I go to on your behalf. Once again I exchange those remarks with Amnon that neither of us remembers the moment after they are made. Once again I try to work out how it might be possible for me to observe as much as I can of what is going to take place. Once again I get up and walk about the house, as if at random, going from room to room in order to see for myself just what their inter-connections are, what views open up from what corners or behind which doors. One important facility I take note of very early is that there is an internal window between Amnon's bedroom and its antechamber; the space is filled with a large stone vase in which are thrust some sprigs of pine, to ornament the room and sweeten the air. Once again I return to my chair, satisfied with what I have seen. A servant brings us a bottle of wine, and we drink from it. Our conversation continues haltingly.

But not for long. Tamar will arrive soon. She will prepare food for Amnon. Amnon will dismiss his servants. He will begin by asking Tamar to nurse and comfort him, but will soon become much bolder with her. Tamar will beg him to let her go. He will warn her that nothing can turn him from his purpose. She will try to save herself by deceiving him. He will seize her. He will rape her.

I will watch.

Yes, Tamar will arrive soon enough.

When she comes she will be shy and eager; voluble and yet uncertain what to say. She will embrace Amnon, greet me with an inclination of her head, stand silently to one side while Amnon tells the old woman accompanying her that she should return to the palace with the litter-bearer; his own servants will see the princess home at the end of her visit.

Tamar will be dressed in a multi-coloured, high-necked dress, its long sleeves buttoned with white coral at the wrists. She will be wearing green eye-shadow of powdered malachite on her lids and in the hollows just beneath her eyes, giving her face a glittering, masked, unfamiliar appearance, like someone about to take part in a ritual or a performance on the stage; her finger and toenails will be painted red. She will look curiously about Amnon's living-room and touch some of his possessions; she will laugh, catching her breath, at a witticism from him or me; then she will insist that he lie down on the couch in the living-room while she goes into the kitchen. She will promise him that she won't be long, and that the food she is going to prepare will make him feel much, much better.

So she will proceed to carry out a request that had been Amnon's own idea, not mine. He had thought the pathos of the request that Tamar should specially cook a meal for him would move both the king and the princess; the simple symbolism of it had, of course, appealed to Amnon himself. Tamar in a giving mood, Tamar feeding him, Tamar satisfying his hungers . . . you get the point, I'm sure. With Tamar in his house at last, however, Amnon will soon show his irritation at having her escape from him so quickly; at seeing her reduce the situation to one of ordinary, placid domesticity. He will shift about on his couch, he will call her to come and sit down, to drink some wine, to tell him the news and gossip he has missed while he's been ill.

'Only when I'm finished,' she will answer from the kitchen, where, gaped at by Amnon's servants, she will go about her culinary duties. I will suspect her, indeed, of taking refuge in those duties from the unfamiliarity of her position. But she will linger in the doorway of the living-room the next time she passes by, and take a glass of wine and drink from it, leaning against the frame of the door. She will have tied her hair back so that it won't be in the way, and with a housewifely providence typical of her she will have brought with her an overall to cover her pretty dress.

She will make pancakes, with a filling of hot, spiced quince, reputed to be very good for the ailing. Vapour of olive oil and yellow batter will rise from one pan; a smell both sweet and pungent from the other, where the grated fruit simmers together with honey, cinnamon and coriander. When each pancake in the skillet is ready, she will favour it with a spoonful of the mixture, and then roll it up and put it together with the others in an earthen-ware dish warming up on the side of the hearth.

We will hear Tamar singing, while she cooks. Will she sing because she feels at ease, or in order to make us think she is at ease?

Then she will come to the door. 'I'm nearly finished. There's just enough batter for a couple more.'

'Haven't you got enough now?'

'No,' she will answer with mock severity. 'And what's more, you're going to eat up every one.'

Finally the cooking will be done. Tamar will have taken great care in arranging the trays which the servants bring in; she will remove her apron so that we can see again how festive is her dress. She will wait at the door, behind the servants, for a word of appreciation from Amnon.

But none will come from him. He will be on his feet, clutching his side as if in pain, stammering out that he suddenly feels faint, he must go to his bedroom, he will eat her food there.

Before going through, however, he will instruct the servants to carry the trays and a couple of small tables into the bedroom. Then he will tell them to go, all of them; he doesn't need them, they must clear out, they must go to their rooms at the other end of the courtyard behind the house. He will turn to me, and speak as if I am no more than another servant. 'And you too, Yonadab. Tamar is here, she will look after me. Just see that they leave, and then you clear out as well. I want some peace.' We will exchange a prolonged glance; his eyes will be steady, expressionless.

I will do as he says, closing the back door behind the last of the servants to leave. I will quench all but one of the lamps in the living-room. I will go to the front door, look behind me to see if I'm being watched, and, having made sure that I am not, I will open the door and slam it loudly. Remaining inside, of course.

The floors are of stone, they will make no sound as your special correspondent takes up his position beneath that internal window to Amnon's bedroom.

Amnon shivers, he tosses his head about the pillow, he complains of the pain he is suffering. No, he can't eat the food she has prepared, nor drink the wine she brings him; perhaps he will be able to do so a little later. But won't she put her hand on his burning forehead? Won't she sit on his bed, so that he can feel her soothing nearness to him?

Can he put his head on her lap, like a child, like the sick child he feels himself to be? Oh, keeping her hand still on his brow, on no account must she take it away.

He lies close to her, his head on her lap, his arms around her waist, spasms of trembling running through him. He murmurs, whispers, snuggles closer to her, still childlike and comfort-seeking. Tamar is diffident but compassionate; perhaps roused a little, without even knowing it; certainly flattered that her powerful brother should have turned to her like an infant. She senses no danger from him: not even when he suggests, with a dry click in his throat, that she should lean back against the headboard of the bed, so that she can be more comfortable. They lie with a blanket between them: it is over him, under her. Her legs are on the floor, to the side of the bed. Now Amnon has lifted his head, he leans it against her breast; his arms still encircle her, holding her more tightly. He looks up and talks to her in a low, urgent voice, never pausing, giving her no time to reflect on what he is saying. He tells her how good she is to him, how he has missed her company during all the weeks of his illness, how he begged their father to allow her to come, how there is no one in the world who can do for him what she is doing. He speaks of the dress she is wearing; of the sweetness of the scent she uses; of her skin, her voice, her hands.

His words become wilder, more incoherent and yet franker too, plainer in their meaning. Everything, he says, starting up abruptly and staring about him, everything in the world is in a process of separation and dissolution; space always going out into more and more space; time passing, never having an end, sick with having no end. But being brother and sister, children of one father, they have the power to roll time back on itself, they can cram distance into their arms and hold it there, if only they dare to. No wonder the world would like to forbid them doing it; no wonder it would use any means to prevent them. That is why, when he looks into her eyes, he sees his annihilation and undoing, and hers too. Yet in her eyes he sees also his redemption and hers from the succession and dispersion that govern the rest of the world. Yes, he and she, because they're brother and sister, born of one father, can together track back time and space to their source, to the original germ from which all things spring.

'You're frightened, Tamar?' he says, looking at her now, his face so close to hers they almost touch. 'But that's right, so you should be, after all the terrors I've been through, because of you. You think my words are mad, you think I'm delirious? I am, I am, I can't deny it. You're the one who's driven me mad. Do you understand me? Are you brave enough to understand me? Don't try to go; I won't let you go; I've only begun to tell you what you are to me. If I don't speak now I shall die.

'And I shall die if I do speak! All right!' But for the moment he doesn't say any more; he lies down and attempts to draw her closer to him.

He has succeeded in frightening Tamar: that is all. She still does not truly understand him, so her alarm is more for him than for herself. She gets up, and he lets her do so; she offers him food and drink, which he again refuses. She is at a loss. She would like to leave him; she feels sorry for him; she is unable to go. She stands at the foot of the bed and tries to pull down the covers and tuck them in. He watches her, with a kind of smile on his lips.

First her incomprehension has to go; then her incredulity.

More words. Some delivered with the air of a crafty lawyer arguing a case in a court of dreams; others babbled and shouted like a bullying child or soldier. 'I know what

I'm saying is forbidden, Tamar, I told you it was. But listen to me, don't shut your ears, don't try to stop me. Forbidden by whom? Whatever the world says, we're the only ones who can really forbid it, no one else. And we're the only ones who can set each other free, just for that reason. If only we dare to! Think what we could become then! Just because we'll have shown that no law and no power can keep us from one another; because we'll have made law and power ours.

'Tamar, I'm asking you to be my wife as well as my sister. Didn't you guess a long time ago how much I love you? I want you: your skin, your hands, your lips, our lips together – what else have I brought you here for, why else have I been sick all this time? Lie with me, Tamar, come, sister, lie with me. I swear you'll never leave this room until you have.'

Now she knows what he wants; how could she not; but still she cannot believe he is in earnest. Not even the fact that he has left the bed and stands at the door like a guard can persuade her that she really is in danger; that he will do anything to her which she forbids him to do. To her? To Tamar, the princess, the king's beloved daughter, the cherished sister of so many stalwart princes? Her disbelief is rooted in her, packed about by her sense of her own value and importance; a bedrock of what could be called innocence, in the circumstances. When she opens her mouth to reproach him, the first absurd complaint she makes is that the food she has prepared for him remains uneaten.

After that first plea, there are others. But Amnon pays no attention to them; Tamar herself is the only audience she has. He stands at the door, blocking it. Every twitch of his lips, every tremor of his hands, every obsessed, downward blink of his eyes, is a fine wedge driven into her belief in her own immunity. So are the reproaches and remonstrances she is uttering, and to which she cannot put a limit once they have begun. Still Amnon is silent; still her voice rises. Her incredulity crazes, cracks, splits, it cannot hold; with a curious, noiseless convulsion that flattens and stretches her features, it disintegrates like so much dust. Perhaps she has just realised that though he does not listen to her cries, he nevertheless welcomes them; they have been assigned to her in all the dreams he has had of this meeting; his sense of his own implacability would be diminished without them. She gestures with an arm, then retracts the gesture hastily, afraid that it might provoke him; she says his name and their father's; she glances hopelessly at the shuttered window. She is like a climber, panting for breath, unable to look ahead or behind her, clinging for long intervals to where she is after each abrupt, tentative move.

Finally the effort is too great for her; she slips, with a single sigh or cry that seems to go on for much longer than her fall. She is on the floor, crouching on all fours, sobbing into her outstretched hands.

'Who will want to marry me? Give me my chance, Amnon. I'm only a girl, don't ruin my life before it's begun. I'm on my knees, isn't that enough? I'll crawl to the door, won't that be enough?' Again and again she says her own name, looking at him or at the floor, 'Tamar . . . I'm only Tamar . . . I'm your Tamar . . .' but it is to remind herself as much as him of her identity that she utters it.

Sitting back on her heels, lifting to him a face that is childishly smeared with tears and green streaks of make-up, she begins to laugh hysterically.

'And you? What will become of you? The whole world will curse you if you touch me. Is that what you want? To

77

shame us all? To be the man who did such a thing to his sister? Nothing else? Only that, always and always?'

Amnon stirs before he speaks. His voice sounds almost calm, after hers. He cannot let her go, he tells her, in the tone of one patiently pointing out some important fact she has overlooked. Not after what he has said to her, and she has said to him. It cannot be. Suddenly he shouts at her: 'It's the words – the *words*, damn you – that are hard! And I've said them. Raping you, killing you, is nothing to me now.'

He runs his hands into his thick black hair and tugs madly at it from both sides, like a man trying to tear his head apart. Then, having hurt himself, he is able to say, quietly once more, and almost with an effect of self-pity, 'I don't want to hurt you, Tamar. Don't make me do it. I want to be gentle with you.'

At once she is on her feet, approaching him with a stiff, fanatical simper on her lips, a crudely unskilled leer. Somewhere, from someone, she has learned to twist her mouth like that, and to turn from the waist, pushing forward and lowering a shoulder to him. Perhaps she has witnessed an exchange between her father and one of his wives or concubines that was never intended for her eyes; or she is just mimicking mimicry, the lewd playfulness of women on their own with nothing better to do.

'Yes,' she says, 'Amnon, I love you too. I know how you feel. I think about you too, when I'm by myself.'

Amnon stares at her incredulously. She comes as close to him as she dares, still talking about the passion she now claims to have had for him; every time she has to pause for breath she remembers to writhe her lips in what is intended to be a coquettish, yielding smile. She has always loved him, she says, best of all her brothers. She never dreamed that one day she'd be able to tell him so. But now they have spoken at last, they can become lovers, real lovers. There is no need for him to shout at her and threaten her.

'Just let me leave you now, Amnon, and tomorrow both of us can go to the king and tell him the truth. He'll change the laws for us, I know he will. Even if he doesn't want to, he'll do it, he'll do anything I ask him. And who can stop him? No one, no one at all. Then there'll be no disgrace, we can marry one another, we'll be able to live together like other husbands and wives. The king won't say no, Amnon. He loves you too, and he wants you to be happy. He wants us both to be happy. He's the king, that's why he's the king, he can arrange everything just as he wants it. Listen to me, let's do what I say, show me that you really do love me by letting me go now. Tonight we can – we can just – we've said – '

Amnon turns away in a movement that might be one of disgust and weariness. The door appears to be unguarded. Tamar lunges at it. With a sweep of his arm, slower and more assured than her dash to escape, he seizes her.

Violence: the last great test of seriousness and sincerity; the irrefutable proof of failure and bad faith. It is both, it is double, it will always be so. Without it, we can achieve nothing; with it, we forfeit the hope of our achievements ever matching our desires.

It was some such truth, I believe, that Amnon and Tamar proceeded to demonstrate. At length. In great detail. Before my burning, watering eyes. Without interruption of any kind.

Apart from the opaque bulge just to the left of me of the vase I have already mentioned, my view was unobstructed. The lighting, though dim, was adequate. The participants in the demonstration were wholly engrossed in their task. I was able to lean against the wall and thus take some of the strain off my feet; even to rest my chin on my clasped hands, which in turn rested on the sill. Sometimes my heartbeat was uncomfortably loud and rapid, high within my throat; sometimes my mouth was so dry I could scarcely move my tongue; at other moments I found my fingers to be wet with the saliva that had dribbled freely on to them. There were times when my loins ached, stirred, even lost a little moisture of their own; or when I had to restrain cries that might have turned into words – though of what kind I do not know – had I permitted them to be uttered; there were passages when I absent-mindedly scratched my cheek or arm, wondered what hour of night it was, and fell into fits of prolonged yawning. Occasionally I wanted to laugh at the absurd inelegance of the spectacle that was being presented to me; or to weep at its deadly earnestness; often I wanted to do both at once.

It was a long night. Had I been less conscientious I might well have abandoned my post. But I didn't. And I won't.

As Amnon grabs her, Tamar swings round, a grimace on her face like a cat's: her nose wrinkled up, her upper lip puckered and rising, her whole face contracting towards the space between her eyes. A gleam of teeth, a darkness of gum, a scream. Amnon's hand goes over her mouth and nose. They face one another, Amnon standing to one side, Tamar jerking her head, trying to free it from his grasp, trying to bite his stifling fingers. Her eyes above his hand are alive with terror and rage; while Amnon gabbles out incoherent words. 'Wait . . . Tamar . . . I mean . . . You must. . . .' Then he yells at her, shaking her head savagely in his grasp. 'You'll spoil it! You're spoiling everything! What's the matter with you?'

In his voice there is a note of genuine indignation; positively of moral reproof. But the irony of it appears lost on Tamar. They stand together, Tamar unmoving now, rigid. Amnon looks into her eyes, and she into his; and it would seem that during that exchange he comes to understand what he has to do, how he can get what he wants. He must hold her, as he is doing, crushed against his body, mouth closed; he can leave her to jerk uselessly against him, to kick with soft-sandalled feet at his ankles; he has to become to her like a storm or a wind, not a person at all, merely an overmastering force which it is hopeless for her to try and resist.

So for a long time he moves only when she compels him to. Their roles are reversed: she is the one who attacks, he is the one who is passive, the resister, the holder-on. He has to be patient: no more than patient. Minutes are contracted into seconds; seconds stretch out into hours. It is like a time of delirium or hallucination; and as in all such dream-states we must assume that in this one, too, there are sounds that strike on their inner ears like bars of music, there are dazzling refractions of light from unknown sources, hurried speeches of great portent and no meaning, flickers of commonplace reason and glimpses of vivid, external details whose ordinariness is the most frightening and inexplicable thing about them; all the heavings and dissolutions of consciousness beyond shame or fear.

Amnon's head sinks forward, his face flattens itself into Tamar's neck. He is holding her up now; if his arms were not around her she would fall. He shifts his weight and hers, not moving from where he stands, and lets his hand drop from her mouth. She does not scream. He sucks at

81

her neck, drawing from it only his own spittle, gulping and swallowing loudly, satisfying an intolerable thirst. Then he picks her up and carries her to his bed. It is easy for him; she is light, there is no strain in his movements. Carrying her against his chest, you might think him to be protective and loving; but his face above is as blind as a fist. He lays her down on the bed; and she starts up at once, stronger for the support she feels beneath her. But he is ready for her, he shoves her back, his hand over her mouth once more. Her body arches, her legs thrash slowly, and he watches them, looking over his own shoulder with a curiosity that passes over his face without changing its expression, as a gleam of light would move across a boulder. One hand bears down with all his weight on her mouth; with the other he whips up her dress. Her legs are revealed to above the knees; they are pale and naked, undulating irregularly, like tendrils in currents of air or water. Amnon sighs, a sound that is louder than Tamar choking for breath under his hand, and the creaking of the bed under the weight of them both.

Time passes. You could not believe there would be so much stillness, so much waiting, so much silence, in the course of a rape. Neither of them has uttered any words since Amnon's last indignant outcry. Their movements are laborious, apparently without purpose. Yet Tamar is now lying on her back, and her legs are exposed. Amnon does not touch them. He watches the shadows that pass and return along them, until with a final weary lift and decline they come to rest flat on the bed. Her knees are together. On a low table there burns a single oil-lamp, the flame floating calmly on the surface of the little lake of oil from which it draws its life. Amnon stares at the flame, wondering whether or not to quench it. Then he looks at his own shadow, hulking upwards to the ceiling. Because the flame is lower than the bed, Tamar's shadow is now entirely swallowed up in that of the bed itself, buried in it.

Yet he waits: perhaps for a sign from her, hoping she might yield and draw him to her, in the end. Or perhaps his cunning still tells him he has nothing to lose, he can only gain, from the passage of time.

Let it pass, then. Limbs split, cracks yawn hugely into shadows that are abolished with a fold of joint upon joint, a closing of bearded lip upon lip where there are no mouths to speak. Amnon has hands to pluck a pillow from the bed and thrust it over her face, to take her dress and petticoats and fling them over her head, to support him as he leans above her to look at what they have exposed, to caress the flesh of her round stomach and oval thighs. Amnon has legs that bear him standing, bear him kneeling, bear him braced like a bridge over her; an expanding and contracting cage of ribs, rivered with hair; round, obtruding buttocks that can stretch and flatten in an instant, racing around curves of their own making to an end already reached; at the fork of his body he has a pendule, a thick bud that must grow, rise, distend, reach and remain stiffly reaching, unable to grasp, fitted at an angle to him yet compelling him to fit himself around it, guiding him who has to guide it, a weapon that disables its wielder; he has a bag of flesh between his legs that does not hang or swing, but clings like a nest of pupae to the rafter of shadow above it. Hands and legs, staff and bag, head and shoulders are between Tamar's legs and over her body; for she has only what he allows her to have, or wills her to have. He blots her out and drags her into being, he rams and drives to create her, he destroys what he makes in his lunge. He swallows her cries in his mouth, her hair is a rope at which he hauls, he lifts her from beneath and thrusts her down from above, he pulls and pushes her, he forces her and eases her, holes her and plugs her. Together they are borne upwards by the burdens they carry into a gyration, a rearing that is a stoop, a surge that sucks them back, a cleaving together that bursts them asunder; their stillness is frenzy, their frenzy is clogged, hard-working, it gasps for air, it threshes for space in which to do away with space.

Do I make it sound obscure? I hope not. There is nothing obscure about it. Brutal, painful, hasty and yet protracted, culminating at last in Amnon's throw of himself as if he would hurl himself over her head but cannot do it because he is caught, rooted fast where he is – and again he hurls himself and is jerked to a halt, again, again, until he rises high above her with a shout and topples sheer down the incline of himself – yes, it is all of these, and it is all plain enough, direct to the point of simplicity; it is what is only to be expected, a limited, predictable arrangement.

And again. Again he gyrates, flexes, arches, lunges; her legs rise and hang unreasonably in the air, wide apart, and are thrown higher by his thrust, and drop, and are thrown up, like flaring wings that lift only themselves, not the locked, heavy bodies on the bed. Just such stretchings are now necessary, such spasms and such indolent, floating pauses, while a pulse beats here, another there. Just such whispers have to crease the air and such cries tear it; and now they have to lie in just such a state of exhaustion, and move their limbs together and apart to writhe across the bedclothes the shapes of such letters from their alphabet or yours.

Amnon is young and strong, goaded by the dread and desire of his life, Tamar is helpless, beaten; what has happened cannot be undone. So she no longer resists him

84

in any way. He has taken the pillow off her head and she does not scream; the dress she was wearing is now lying on the floor. He rests between her legs and over her; then he is unable to rest and begins once more. Later he rests across her, his head dangling towards the floor. How many times in the course of the night he rouses himself from spells of complete inertness to fling himself into her again I do not know. Many times: driven still to reach a point that he seeks within her only because it is beyond his uttermost touch. Still beyond. Just beyond. Always beyond.

7

In other words, when all was done, it was 'just another fuck'.

The words, I hasten to add, are Amnon's, not mine. They were said to his sister when he drove her out of his house the next morning. He uttered them in an absolute paroxysm of moral outrage, as if *he* was the one who had been assaulted and betrayed.

'If you knew what I've been through!' he screamed at her; at least, it sounded like a scream, though his voice never rose above a whisper. 'If you knew what I've suffered! For what?'

Then, for the first time, he said the words I quoted a moment ago; he was to repeat them many times in the next few minutes.

Just another fuck! Eloquent phrase! Say what you like, Amnon deserves to be called a man of the highest and most inflexible principle. It wasn't any common guilt or remorse made him turn on Tamar; but disappointment. Definitely, disappointment. He ravened in it, this baffled, stark naked idealist; this thirster after the divine; this bringer together of time and eternity, of the mundane and the transcendent; this lover of his sister. Accommodation and compromise were not for him; not then; not in his rage at the renewed discovery of his own unmodified, incurable, inglorious humanity.

How could poor Tamar compete with him? She had even dared to smile at him, when he had first got up and stood over her, as the lamp guttered and died and the shadows it had thrown were replaced by larger, vaguer shadows falling at different angles into different corners of the room from a source of light hitherto unseen. Her smile was timid, propitiatory, nothing more than a flicker of the lips, a signal of submission and a plea for recognition. Yet its meaning had been unmistakeable: to me as well as to Amnon. Tamar, after all, was a pragmatist. Perhaps she had inherited the talent for it from her father. There was no point in crying over spilt milk or a split hymen. What had been done to her could not be repaired or forgotten; and for that very reason she was prepared to try to make the best of it, somehow. One might almost say that, in a mood utterly different from Amnon's, she was ready to agree with his description of what had passed between them. Who knows, perhaps the proposal she had made earlier, merely as a ruse to escape from him, could now become a fact, a policy, a way out of the disgrace and humiliation into which she had been thrust.

Her smile, anyway, was game, pragmatic, entirely female. The man of principle met it with a look of hatred so intense his face grew not darker but lighter, gleaming in the sweat that rose to his skin. Suspended over the bed, as forked and fissured as a satyr, as tremulous as a spider

86

hanging from its own web, he called her a whore, a slut, a bitch, a cow, a hole, a thing. She disgusted him, he told her, he didn't know how he'd been able to bring himself to touch her.

And more. Much more. 'Out! Out!' he whispered, scurrying about the floor for her clothes and flinging them at her. 'And I thought. . . . How could I have imagined? . . . Another world! And nothing there! You go to the end of everything, you risk everything. . . . Just another fuck! Look at it, look at it lying there!' He gesticulated, showing his teeth, and struck himself savagely against the side of his head. Tamar's dress flew wildly through the air, almost performing a cartwheel as if in manic high spirits, before coming to rest across her face. He pulled the dress away in order to thrust into her face his own, labouring with the fury his words could not express. 'What are you waiting for? You want the servants to come and throw you out? You think you're the first whore they've had to throw out of here?'

If he was going to call the servants, clearly it was time for me to be gone. Before I left, however, Tamar spoke up; and for the first time her moral force was more than equal to her brother's. I marvelled at how much older she had grown during the night, or perhaps just in the course of the morning that had scarcely begun. Under the renewed violence of his abuse she had cried heartbrokenly – surprising me, for I had thought her to be long past tears; she had lain quite still, curled over, with her hands covering her head; she had stuck her fingers into her ears. Now, sitting up and gathering her clothes into a heap in front of her naked bosom, she spoke without anger, almost without hatred, certainly without any hope of making him change towards her; she spoke for the sake of the truth alone, and then said no more.

'What you are doing now, Amnon, is even worse than what you did to me last night.'

Whereupon my remarkable cousin Amnon gave vent to a series of exclamations of disgust and contempt of a kind almost impossible to imitate or transliterate: *Ekh*, *pfeh*, *tchah*, and suchlike. It was with these sounds in my ears that I crept as quietly as I could out of the house and into the lane.

Jerusalem is a city of stone, built upon stony hills. Water runs away swiftly from it, but light lingers, light clings to the stones, or comes out from them, so that even at the darkest hour of the night you see patches of pallor at your feet; they rise up to your hand when you put it out to support yourself against a wall; they loom above you if you look up from the lower streets to the higher. With the coming of dawn it seems that the stones already contain within themselves all the colours you will see during the passage of the day, from the first grey that fills the eastern sky to the last orange glow there will be in the west just before nightfall; with every dry glaring yellow of midday, bronze of afternoon, or pink of sunset, held there unchanging, foreknown and remembered.

So with the day – beginning again, entrapped in stone before it has begun – into which Tamar emerges.

She has been ravished and thrown into the street by her ravisher, her brother. Yet the day is an ordinary one, just like any other. It is up to her, then, to transform the day, to transcend it, to make it yield her a meaning commensurate with what she has undergone. She knows her suffering to be beyond absorption or assimilation into any life she had previously been able to conceive for herself; the secret shame within the larger shame she feels is that she attempted to make it do so.

That is past. Now she will assimilate the rest of her life to this event; she will stand by it and judge herself wholly by it; she will make of it the absolute that Amnon had wanted it to be. Her ambitions, though, are more precise than his. She will take her revenge on him, and reclaim her pride from its own wreckage.

With her back against a wall of stone, her feet bare on the pavement, Tamar, the princess, who looks so much like any other girl, gazes about an ordinary street, revealed in the light of a common summer's dawn. No one else is about, though some smoke has begun to rise into the air from a few of the low, shuttered houses near by. There is no wind, not even the faintest of breezes, so each stream of smoke rises steadily, coiling round and round upon itself as it goes, as if ascending an insubstantial spiral stairway of its own making.

Still she hesitates. Among other, greater fears, it seems, she is afraid of rupturing the tenuous yet solemn silence of the morning; she is held back by a compunction or timidity of a kind that must appear trivial even to her, and that yet reaches into the depths of her being. Besides, this girl who looks so much like any other, has never before actually stood alone in a public street. All she knows of the city is what she has seen when she has passed through it in her litter, covered over so carefully that not a sign of her within has been visible to others, as if it were the ark of the Lord the litter-bearers were carrying.

Yet, to the shame and indignity she has already suffered, she has to add more: for her, honour lies beyond a further degradation that she has to bring upon herself. She cannot creep home, hoping to remain unobserved, or pretending to the palace guards nothing is amiss; she cannot take her secret into those rooms of hers which will never again look to her as they did the day previously, because she herself has changed so much; she cannot meet her father and brothers and try to pass herself off as the spoiled, innocent princess she had always been. She cannot even go straight to them with her tale. Her pride, her passion for revenge, and even more, her determination to impose her own unalterable order upon the disorder that has overwhelmed her, all demand that she show herself, bedraggled and bloody in a torn dress, to the whole city. She has to make sure that there is no one in Jerusalem who does not hear what has happened to the only daughter of King David. The crowd must come running to their doors and windows to gawk and laugh at the wretchedness of their princess; her own voice must tell them what has been done to her; her own hands must heap ashes and filth on her head. If she is no longer the untouchable, unviewable, immaculate princess, if she can now never become the bride of a king, the queen of an unknown country, bringing with her a dowry of provinces, she can still offer herself as a spectacle and warning for the country to wonder at; as the heroine-victim of the drama which she herself will make public.

But the price of it! Not just of the hours she is about to go through in the streets of Jerusalem; but of the months and empty years to follow. She hesitates; yet does she have any sense of how long those years will be? How can she realise what it will be like to watch day after day like this one arrive, while she, true to the role she has chosen, remains the ruined, honourable princess, tied for ever to a disgrace and redemption that have no body or life; that life, indeed, can only erode and make unreal even to her, as the years pass? Certainly, she can expect at first to be an object of awe and pity among those she will have to live with. But later – ? A source of scurrilous gossip and recollection merely; and later still of sheer incredulity – incredulity that that thick-bodied yet withered spinster, that unfruitful old woman, without husband or children but with many fussy ways and ridiculous habits, was once sought after, pursued, madly ravished for the sake of a beauty no one can imagine her ever having possessed. Does she see her nephews and nieces, and eventually their children too, looking sideways at her . . . at Aunt Tamar, an invaluable help around the houses of others, never her own, in which she is compelled to live; given to favouritism among the young; bitterly vindictive towards girls who get into trouble, yet with a curiously prurient softness towards the men who do it to them? Does she understand that that too is the part she is assigning herself? And that each of the days which take so long to pass will fall away neither into memory nor true forgetfulness, but merely into a vague, ever-present sense of loss, of having been cheated, of having done all that could have been asked of her and of yet having been found insufficient?

No, even though Tamar hesitates, shivering with fear and cold, shrinking back from the future which she is about to bring on herself, it is impossible that she should realise just what that future will be.

But let us give her the benefit of the doubt. Let us say that even if she could know what is to become of her, even if she could feel in one contracted, intolerable pang all the nullity and dreariness of the years ahead, she would still open her mouth, as she does now, to tell the city of the crime committed against her.

Honour . . . shame. . . . Do I irritate you and make you feel restless by talking of these? If so, I can't say that I feel much inclination to apologise for it. Honour and shame, you would perhaps like to tell me, are notions or emotions you are simply unable to take very seriously; and the same, *a fortiori*, goes for pride of birth or position, and for a concern over sexual chastity (of all things!), and for the rest of the sanctions and moral imperatives by which we benighted folk were supposed to live in our day. True, even the most conscientiously enlightened among you would probably grant that rape and incest together make an unsavoury combination; you would agree that they reek of criminality, or at least of the gravest degree of social maladjustment. But still, you would be sensible about them, wouldn't you, not like poor Tamar, that idiot-girl who now stands with her back against a wall, trying to gather strength for the first cry which she hopes will appal her hearers as much as it appals her to utter it. As for the transcendental ambitions that so inflamed Amnon, his pursuit of the magical powers imputed to whatever is forbidden – such antic (and antique) hopes and frenzies are surely not for you. None of them. Where can they lead, if not ultimately to God in his white beard issuing absurd injunctions about marriage and consanguinity and what foods to eat and a host of other details which you sincerely trust I will be good enough to spare you?

Yes, I know how you feel. I agree with you in many ways. I am myself a little embarrassed at having such matters brought up, and at seeing them taken so seriously by my family and friends. Which is precisely why I am not in the least inclined to apologise for thrusting them upon you. Understand, I cannot have any more respect for your enlightenment (or scepticism, if you so prefer) than I have for my own. Knowing myself, knowing the emotions I have had to put up with inside myself, I see no reason whatsoever to suppose that you are any more liberated than I am from pride or shame; or than Tamar is from self-importance; or Amnon is from a longing for self-transcendence; or David from hunger for the esteem and admiration of others; or Absalom from notions of personal honour. I grant that the modes of expressing these, the areas in which it is believed they are to be found, the manner of pursuing or fleeing from them, change radically, almost unrecognisably, with changing times and countries: that's so obvious the point hardly seems worth making. But must I therefore cease to speak of them? Must I flatter the notion you like to have of your difference from the miserable, weightless rabble who crowd the spaceless chambers and corridors of the dead? Not as long, comrades, as you cling to that very belief in your difference from us, which is no more than a manifestation of your particular style of self-importance. Not as long as you make your grabs at transcendence through history, love, art, the fate of the nation or the proletariat, the smoking of hashish, or even the watching of television. Not as long as you revel in the admiration of the people around you and shuffle with whatever truths you claim to believe out of fear of their disapproval; or continue to show yourself as one man to your wife, another to your friend, a third to an enemy who is stronger than you, a fourth to an enemy who is weaker. Not as long as your 'generation' – to use the word you love so much – continues to fulfil in its own way, like every other, its varying norms of conformism and credulity.

And if you say to me that, standing where I do, I cannot afford to proclaim anything else – well, I won't deny it. I will only ask you to reflect a little on some of the things you can't afford.

Enough of Yonadab's wisdoms. Let's get back to that dawn, that wall, that girl. Let the girl open her mouth again, and let me refrain from interrupting her this time.

93

Her first utterance is no more than a low moan. Yet only then, after she has managed to send her voice ahead of her, as it were, is she able to move.

She does not go far, just a few paces. She falls silent, and turns her head to look at the house from which she has been thrust out. It is blind, its doors are locked, according to the instructions given by Amnon to his servants. She moves further away from it. Then she runs across the lane to the house immediately opposite to where she was standing and beats with her fist against the door.

'Open up! Open the door!'

Her voice is thin, without power or conviction. The hysteria she needs has not yet mastered her or set her free; she is still without the strength that will be given to her by the presence of the audience she is calling for. She doesn't wait to be answered; she leaves that house and runs some distance down the lane, stumbling on her bare feet over the uneven cobbles. She halts, limps to another door, bangs on it and again cries for it to be opened to her.

You would think she would get an immediate response; but people are slow to be roused from their sleep; they are perhaps frightened or incredulous. It is only after she has knocked on the fourth or fifth door that there are the first answering cries of alarm, and a clatter of windows opening to her. Out of them stare men and women with startled, blinking eyes and uncombed hair, their clothes thrown around their shoulders and held in place by clutching hands. One family, another, a woman servant carrying a water-jar, an old man in his doorway with a stick raised to fight off the band of intruders he imagines to be in the street. It is on him that Tamar advances; he raises his stick still higher and retreats into his house. She falls to her knees in front of him and grovels on the ground. Outside the house, in the gutter, is a pile of refuse of all kinds, household rubbish, shit, scraps of food thrown out for the dogs and chickens to scratch through and carry away; there is a pile of ashes too, among the rest, and Tamar seizes a handful of it and pours it on her head, in the ancient gesture of mourning. Awkwardly, as if it is a trick she still has to learn, she bends lower and strikes her head against the edge of the gutter.

'I am Tamar,' she tells the old man. 'I am the daughter of the king. My brother has raped me. Ruined me, and thrown me out of his house.'

The old man immediately slams the door in her face.

She turns away, and sees how many people there now are in the lane. A bruise is already rising on the tender skin of her forehead, where she struck it against the kerb. There is fear and bewilderment in the onlookers' eyes; in hers the dry, staring light of a will she can know only as a power holding her, moving her, directing her towards the consummation it has chosen her to fulfil. To the crowd she appears to be demented; but though her dress is torn and to the dirt that was on it before there have been added dribbles of grey and black ash, everyone sees from her clothing that she is a woman of rank, of the palace, one of the king's women. For both reasons the people thronging together in the narrow lane don't dare to come too close to her; when she starts forward they scatter, leaving a pathway for her to go through. Then she walks slowly and stiffly along the path, halting in front of this man or that to explain and expose herself to him. Now that her audience is so much closer to her she does not raise her voice; at the end of each utterance she nods her head earnestly, childishly, to impress on her listeners the importance of what she is telling them.

The speech she makes is always the same. She is the

king's daughter, Tamar. Her brother Amnon has raped her, ruined her, and thrown her out of his house, into the street. She is the king's daughter, Tamar. Her brother Amnon has raped her. She begged him to set her free, but he was stronger than she, and he raped her. She is the king's only daughter, Tamar.

Stopping here and there, moving on, talking always, she comes to an open space, a small piazza where four streets meet, with steps leading up or down to each. Below her is an irregular, pallid patchwork of walls and flat rooftops, spread out and contracted, hung about with washing-lines and dotted at random with storage-jars and drying melons on the roofs. The terraces of buildings are interrupted by unbuilt-upon ridges and outcrops of stone, by the dark incisions of alley-ways running at angles to one another, by the black, coin-like circles of cisterns, all waiting for the sun. Above, there is the wall of the palace, bright where the first rays of sunlight have already fallen on it, mauve within its shadowed abutments and embrasures. Tamar has been going downhill, away from the palace; she now hesitates in the middle of the piazza, looking up, but finally takes one of the flights of steps leading farther down. Beneath the steps is one of the poorest quarters of the town, where the houses aren't of stone or are made only partly of stone, patched together with mud, sun-dried bricks, and branches of trees, and where the lanes are merely trodden pathways. Then there is a street of tradesmen's booths, some already being opened for the day, others still deserted. On every corner people run to see Tamar pass, or wait where they are; they stare, they point, they jump up and down to have a better glimpse of her. Some shout out that she's a sorceress, a whore, a drunkard, the victim of an assault by a platoon of soldiers; others babble of Amnon, of Tamar, of the king's anger; everyone knows that she is of high rank, she is connected with the palace and the king, and that what they are witnessing is altogether out of the ordinary, an overturning of the natural order of events. All feel themselves to be participants in the drama, necessary to it, privileged to be so. Yet when she halts to tell them yet again who she is and what has been done to her, they cannot meet her gaze; they look down guiltily, afraid of being implicated, perhaps recognised later. It makes no difference to Tamar. She speaks to each of her listeners as though he has been chosen to hear the words which are specially intended for him.

At last, when the rays of the sun have penetrated into the valley, she begins to climb towards the palace, followed by a jostling, yelling crowd. Of the geography of the city she knows no more than that her home is above the rest of it, that she will find it if she labours uphill long enough. Once she is on her way home, however, she starts to run, she no longer halts to talk to single people, she doesn't utter words but shrieks out meaninglessly, she tears at her hair with ash-blackened hands. By chance, on her way up she takes the lane that leads past Amnon's house, but no one comes out of it to see her go by and she does not recognise it. The house is just one among so many others; the street is just another ascending, cobbled stretch of the way she has to traverse before reaching her home.

But the palace was no longer her home.

No one, I swear, could ever have anticipated that Tamar would find it easier to tell a mob of strangers what had happened to her than to break the news to her father. I am sure Tamar herself, so far as she was conscious of her own actions, was astonished to find that she could not go to him. She tried, we saw her try, and she could not do it.

Now, I suppose, there is no alternative for you but to regard what she did as inevitable, logical, and even (in retrospect, of course) as perfectly predictable. She must come to the palace-gate; she must stare despairingly up at it, while the soldiers on duty shout at her from above; she must come closer to the gate and put out a hand to touch it, or to prevent herself from falling; she must turn and flee in the direction of Absalom's house.

Doubtless, it wasn't only because of her fear and shame before the king that she turned away from him. He had failed her. He had sent her to Amnon; therefore, like a child, she would blame him for all that had followed.

But who, watching her then, could have predicted that David would interpret her pathetic flight from him as an unforgivable insult, and would believe that she chose deliberately to regard Absalom as her protector, as the more powerful man to appeal to?

(Yet that response of David's, too, in retrospect, will appear to have been inevitable.)

So we will never know what would have happened if, even after having exposed herself to the streets, she had gone to her father with her story. Much would have been different; that is all we can say.

She went to Absalom. Hence she would never again be allowed to pass through the palace gates. She and David were never to meet again.

8

Absalom. The glamour boy of the court. With his long hair and long legs; his hazel eyes and broad chest; his deep voice and self-regarding smile; his way of standing with his head bent a little to one side, as if he were silently, and with becoming modesty, receiving the applause of an admiring crowd. He'd had enough practice at it, to be sure.

Forgive the malice and facetiousness of my tone. It's a sign of embarrassment. I never found it easy to strike the right note with Absalom, or about him. I always felt uncomfortable in my dealings with him. I suppose, really, I was always a little frightened of him. That feeling hasn't entirely left me, it would seem, even though he is now utterly powerless to do me any harm, while there is plenty that I can do to him. With my tongue, at least.

Frightened? I don't think I exaggerate. But it's difficult to describe the quality of the fear he roused in me, or to give an adequate explanation of it. It's true that (as you will see) Absalom once sent a gang of his strong-arm boys to kidnap me and drag me before him; then he took out a knife, put it against my throat and threatened to saw my head off. But the fear I felt then, though intense enough, was also of the most elementary kind. Whereas the fear I felt of him before the kidnapping, and which I continued to feel long after the incident had been supposedly forgotten in the warmth of our subsequent, newfound friendship, was always obscure and irritating.

Let me put it this way. On the whole I don't have much trouble in identifying myself temporarily, in one fashion or another, with most of the people in this story; or at any rate, in pretending to myself that had I been given a character different from the one I actually have, or had my circumstances been different from what they actually were, I might well have felt and behaved as they did. Indeed, there are times when I suspect myself never to have been anything more than a mind inhabited by other minds, a kind of counterfeit personality, whose ability to manipulate others was achieved only at the cost of, or was the direct result of, a permanent self-impoverishment, a never-ending haemorrhage of inner identity.

None of this, however, applies to Absalom. He was alien to me, incomprehensible, always at a remove. The paradox is that he appeared to me in this light *not* because he was so complicated, but because he was so simple. I could never figure out how he managed it. It had (and has) me beat. Absalom was ambitious, self-confident, vain, and idealistic; he was always ambitious, self-confident, vain, and idealistic; he appeared to take his character or characteristics to bed with him every night and to get them up every morning unrumpled by dreams, irony, boredom, or self-doubt. I would have sworn he perspired self-confidence, pissed vanity, shat ambition, shot idealism into his women. What, I ask you, can a man like myself do with such an animal? Except to admit that he doesn't understand him and is a little afraid of him.

To be tall and beautiful, to be envied, to be admired, to know that great things are expected of you, *and* to be convinced that you intend to use your gifts only for the good of others – what an unbeatable combination! No wonder Absalom's head was turned. No wonder that the crowd, the masses, the man in the street, loved him above all the other princes; and that he in turn was always ready to confess to a passionate admiration for the man in the street. Not as the man in the street actually was, but as he could be, one day, if he were given his chance. By Absalom, among others.

For Absalom was – excuse me – a progressive. He was a hater of injustice. An enemy of established authority of every kind, not least that of his father and the priests. A friend of the poor. A bold planner of schemes for the redistribution of land, new codes of law, new methods of government. A maximiser of happiness. A firm believer in the future which would surely see all these things come to pass. Indeed, what made him above all else a true progressive in my eyes was his conviction that the future he was so dedicated to would somehow retrospectively balance up or cancel out all the evils and pains of the past; it would give meaning to them, prove them to have been ultimately worthwhile. It goes almost without saying that that would apply in particular to any evils Absalom himself might have to commit in order to bring the future about.

This was a point of view I could never begin to understand, quite candidly. It seems more than ever senseless to me now that I stand here, divided from you and united to you by all the time that has passed since Absalom's death and my own. Do not flatter yourselves, my dears, that anything you do will diminish by one iota the pains we felt when we were able to. Do not imagine that generations succeeding yours will be able to redeem you from your failures and misfortunes. Take it from me: each of us bears his own burden forever. For as much of forever as he is allowed to know.

Anyway, Absalom's attachment to the idea of all that was yet to come gives me my sanction to indulge in the longest anticipation of the future (that is now also part of the past) which I have so far permitted myself. I invite you to look at the end of Absalom's own public and private future: the very end, I mean, long after the murder of Amnon and my own departure – 'under a cloud', as they say – from the court. I mean the last day of Absalom's life, when he knew that his long drawn out rebellion against his father had finally failed.

Alone, mounted on a bedraggled mule, the confusion of the battlefield behind him and sanctuary in the country of his mother's kinsmen three hopeless days' ride ahead, David's troops searching for him in every thicket and his own broken followers ready to turn him in if they could purchase pardon for themselves by doing so – no, not even Prince Absalom would have been able to tell himself then that the events of the day and all his actions leading up to it would ultimately be to the benefit of mankind and his own greater glory, and that he was still the king's favoured son, the time's favoured son, the favoured son of the nation yearning for him to deliver it from his father's palsied rule. For Absalom, the not entirely unprecedented consciousness of failure, the indignity and squalor of it, the knowledge that the path he was following was one he had been compelled to take once before and that this time there was no possibility of a come-back, must have been even more tormenting, I am convinced, than thirst or hunger, fear or weariness.

So I imagine him making his way along the western bank of the Jordan, heading north, upstream, towards Geshur: swaying, half-conscious, looking out for pursuers when he remembered to, sobbing when he could, cursing himself for having listened to the advice of Hushai and of having thus delivered his forces to their defeat (did he suspect then that Hushai had all the time been in clever

David's pay?), kicking in spasms at the belly of his mule whenever he had enough energy to do it.

That mule of his: also a character in the story. With longer ears than any other. It, too, had had a hard day; a day of fear, noise, blows, insufficient food and water. In its mulish brain or nervous system there can have been just one mule's version of an idea. It was being made to work; it was being driven farther and farther from the fields and stable it recognised as home; the kicking creature on its back was responsible for its sufferings: therefore, it had to get rid of him. So it did what mules and horses have been doing ever since men first got on their backs: today, too, if you are out of luck in the mount given to you at a livery stable you may get a brute who will try the same trick on you, quite unaware that times and techniques have changed so greatly, and that for you riding is a sport, a pleasure, not a serious means of locomotion. Absalom's mule waited until the path they were following ran near a tree that had an overhanging branch of the right height; then with a duck and swerve of its back, so subtle you wouldn't believe a horse or mule to be capable of it unless you have felt that particular lithe, sickening movement beneath you, it was off the track and under the tree, dragging its rider with it.

The mule had chosen better than it could have known. The branch was not one, but two. Some knot or quirk in the trunk had determined that a pair of branches should grow like two limbs pressed together, parallel to one another, in a deformation almost human in appearance, arthritically so, good reason for groaning when the wind is high. The first branch, the first blow, did not unseat Absalom; it was the second that took him, just when he may have thought, if he knew what was happening to him, that he was through safely. The branch parted a little from its brother; one can imagine how stiffly and yet how swiftly; then came back, as it had to, to its old resting place. But it could not find it. For now, held fast between the two branches, pegged between them, was Absalom's head.

The mule slithered, stumbled, broke through the undergrowth and turned, bridle hanging loose, in the direction in which it imagined its home to lie. We may doubt, in view of the numbers of soldiers from both armies scrambling about in the valley, that it ever reached the home it was looking for. Absalom, third son of the king, most popular of the princes, rebel, man of action and seeker after a better future for us all, was left dangling, his feet high off the ground, his head trapped but not crushed. He hung and was unable to fall, the original *luftmensch*, his own weight remorselessly dragging him towards the earth from which he was held free. Time hung with him, suspended, drawn through itself to no end, as he was; unable to win for itself the extinction for which it strained. Only his cells must have burst and cracked in the vacancy, the cords of his swinging body were stretched to sustain him, he had become his own rack.

Then the news was brought to cousin Joab, commander of David's army, riding by with a group of his officers. Ghastly cries, like those of a beast, had been heard; those who had followed the cries had seen a man hanging between the branches of a tree; a man dressed in the clothes and armour of a prince; a man whose loosened hair was so long and thick it covered the branches where they held him fast. It was the king's son; it could be no one else; he must have tried to take his own life and failed in that endeavour too.

One can understand Joab's irritation at hearing the report. How much more convenient it would have been for him if the accident that had befallen the prince had killed him outright, or if the excited fools who had brought the news had taken it on themselves to finish him off. Now the job still had to be done. Grimy, grey-haired, corpulent in the saddle, his eyes swollen and inflamed with the sights of yet another battlefield he had mastered, Joab yelled at them, 'You should have killed him! I'd have paid you if you'd done it! Why didn't you do it?'

No, they replied, huddling together and retreating. Never. How could they? Everyone knew that the king had said that he wanted the prince taken alive.

Joab knew it too. But he did not hesitate for long. He had killed too many of the king's enemies – against the expressed wishes of the king – to be afraid of adding this one to his score. He still held his position as commander of the army: which was the best way he had of judging what the real wishes of David were. None of the others he had despatched, it was true, had been a son of the king; but that made little difference to Joab. Especially as he had a private grudge against Absalom. He had been the one who had twice interceded with the king on Absalom's behalf, after the killing of Amnon; he had begged the king to overlook the ferocity and guile with which Absalom had avenged the rape of his sister, and to allow him to return to Jerusalem. And how had he been repaid for the trouble he had taken?

So he rode over to see the spectacle, regarded it from some distance for a while, then dismounted. Out of a saddle-pouch he took three small, weighted darts. The other officers watched him from where they had drawn up their horses, in an open, grassy place much littered with sheep and goat droppings, where in quieter times the animals grazed and lay for shelter against the wind. Some of the onlookers said later that Absalom heard the approach of the group, and struggled desperately to set himself free, flailing his useless legs in the air and clawing at the branches which held him. Others were to say that he did not move; that his consciousness had long since been crushed out of him.

All agree, anyhow, that Joab was unhurried and business-like. Carefully, having come to a halt at the right distance from Absalom, he balanced his own weight for a moment, before plunging forward with one of the iron-tipped darts. The blow went home, the point found its gap in Absalom's armour. His legs contracted upwards, his knees came up to his stomach, like an infant's; his body swung sideways. When it came back the next dart was ready; Joab was poised for his second blow. Only when the third went in did Absalom's legs slowly relax, stretch downwards, as if in weariness. Yet, when they hauled the branches apart and the prince dropped in a blood-laced heap on the ground, he was still alive. He clutched with both hands at the earth he hadn't been able to reach before.

Joab turned away, leaving to his underlings the merciful task of finishing what he had begun. Then he told his trumpeter to sound the signal for his troops to leave pursuing the rebels and to lay down their arms; and the signal was taken up from one company to the next, for many miles down the valley. The rebellion, that can be said to have begun the very morning after Amnon's rape of Tamar, was at last over.

Loudly mourning for his son, the king returned to Jerusalem, determined that Joab, who had murdered the murderer, should meet his murderers, too, when the time was ripe.

That's the way it goes with princes. The rest of us may dream of rising up in revolt against our stupid, embarrassing, unenlightened parents and rulers, of doing away with the tyranny and caprice of their authority over us, of establishing a new reign of justice and candour in the world, and, in the same blow, of securing our fame as heroes and liberators. But how do we non-princes generally translate our dreams into reality? By slamming doors; by arguing over money and the use of the family sedan (car or chair, as the case may be); by swearing at our elders when we are among our friends and imitating their idiotic manners and turns of speech; by wearing clothes which we know they will dislike; by making unsuitable marriages; by flaunting (when it is reasonably safe to do so) our membership of radical political organisations. Unsatisfactory means, most of them: confessions of impotence, mockers of our own intentions, occasions for malicious comment by outsiders.

With princes, real princes, the case is altered. Kingdoms, dynasties, laws, systems of belief, armies, their own lives and the lives of entire populations: these are what they put at stake, these are the issues they engage.

Amnon, too; I haven't been speaking in the present case just with Absalom in mind. Not at all. In some ways, I confess, Amnon's rebellion actually seems to me more radical than his brother's; more dangerous, more unpredictable in its consequences, more of a lunge into the unknown.

For when I look at a rebel like Absalom, a man who gave his life to overthrow his father's outworn reign, I see him as his father's most determined and reckless enemy, certainly; but I can't help seeing him also as the very man of all those around David who was most impressed by what David had accomplished, most in awe of David's position, the one who could think of nothing more important in his life than to seize that position for himself.

The man, in short, who wanted to *be* David. With differences, of course: it would be Absalom on the throne, not David, and he would be a good king, a wise king, a reforming king, a king beloved by the people for whose benefit only he would rule. Differences of that order. But king nevertheless, just like the daddy he would have to kill in order to become king.

Ach, I admit that my attitude in such matters may be considered less an attitude than an incapacity: a disease, as I've already called it. I can't really blame Absalom for regarding me with as much suspicion as I regarded him, and with very much more contempt.

But I'm not complaining. There's nothing that can be done about it now. Besides, like most other non-princes I have (or had) my consolations. At least I didn't end up hanging from a tree with Joab sticking javelins into my side. Having been compelled to leave the court after Amnon's death, as I've already mentioned, I retired to the country and so managed to avoid taking sides in Absalom's rebellion and several subsequent upheavals; unlike most of the others mentioned in this story, I was able to live a long, relatively untroubled, if somewhat boring life. I had property, my neighbours treated me with a proper degree of deference, I was not dissatisfied with the wives I managed to procure, those of my children who survived their babyhood grew up to be respectable citizens. My death, when it came, was both expected and regretted by all who knew me. It wasn't even too uncomfortable a death, as these things go. I fell ill, shivered and cried for a few days, plagued more by dreams and chills than by pain, and then it was all over. Over and done for: except for appearances such as this.

Then let's get on with it. Where was I? Oh yes, Absalom's death and its connection with Amnon's very dissimilar rebellion, which is my real subject; the one about which I can claim to be the world's greatest dead authority. What really concerns me here is to say no more than that it was over Amnon and Tamar that Absalom was forced to present his first direct, bloody challenge to the king. From that challenge all else in his short life followed: the period after the death of Amnon which he was forced to spend in exile – where we will not follow him; the plotting and planning he indulged in immediately he was permitted by the king to return to Jerusalem – which is not my business; the final abortive *coup d'état* – of which you have seen as much as you need to. No doubt you are entitled to say that he would sooner or later have found some other occasion for making his challenge, if the affair of Amnon and Tamar hadn't come up. But that was the occasion he found, or that was presented to him by Tamar, so it's the one he has to stick to now, whether he likes it or not. And the rest of us with him.

9

So Tamar may begin once again. Everything is now ready for her; just as it was – just as it has to be – the morning after the rape. Here is Absalom, standing in the street outside the gate to his house. Here is the mob that has been following her about. And here I am, keeping within earshot but hanging well back, with my cloak about my face.

Tamar sees we are all in position and waiting for her.

Amnon, she then declaims, has raped her. He had pretended to be ill and had asked the king to send her to him, to prepare food for him; once she was in his house he had dismissed his servants and bolted the door; he had then assaulted her; he had held her prisoner throughout the night; he had assaulted her repeatedly. She had begged and pleaded to be released; she had warned him to let her go; she had reminded him who she was and who he was; she had called on God, on the law, on her father, on her brothers, to save her. Nothing had helped. In the morning he had thrown her out of the house, he had called his servants and told them to turn her into the street – as she was, as Absalom now saw her, as the whole city had seen her. Yes, the whole city, through which she had just made her way: exposed, undone, a spectacle to them all. She had no secrets from the mob now.

Then let there be no secrets between themselves and the mob if Absalom should choose to turn her away. She could not enter his house until she had told him all that had happened to her; before she passed through his door she had to give him the choice of accepting or rejecting her. Let Absalom look at her before he spoke; let him ask himself if he was still ready to acknowledge his kinship to her and to give shelter to a creature who would never be anything but a reminder of the vileness of which she had been victim. She would not protest or reproach him if he declined to open his house to her. There were stones enough in Jerusalem to dash out her brains; high places enough for her to leap from; deserts close enough in which she could perish from hunger and thirst; wild dogs and leopards enough to tear her limbs apart; tribesmen enough to carry her across the river as their slave.

Thus – more or less – Tamar to Absalom. Having been unable to tell her story to her father, she has chosen to make what you might vulgarly call a big production of her confrontation with Absalom. By insisting (solely in order to give him a free choice in the matter, of course) that he come out to her in the street, she has secured the services of an audience of several hundred extras; and her rhetoric is directed towards them quite as much as towards Absalom. Yet you would be mistaken if you should therefore conclude that her hyperbolic words and histrionic gestures are necessarily insincere; and that, if she were put to it, she would really flinch from those high cliffs, wild beasts, deserts and so forth. Such highflown display is now the only mode of self-expression open to her; she can adopt no other.

Equally, you would not be mistaken in suspecting her of having made it very difficult for Absalom to do anything but lead her into his house and give her the shelter and comfort she earnestly proclaims she is ready to do without. Cunning Tamar, daughter of David! How intricate sincerity can be among those who have a genuine gift for it! Your ordinary hypocrite, like my father, doesn't stand a chance among such people. Absalom himself would be altogether outclassed, were it not that he has a gift of his own which serves him quite as well as his sister's sincerity serves her; he has his vanity.

So when he finally stirs from the shocked impassivity with which he has listened to her, vaguely and doubtfully frowning, like a blind man with his face turned towards the sun – when he stirs, he goes directly to what he, if not she, has seized upon as a central issue.

'Does the king know all this?'

'No. I've come straight to you.'

Absalom breathes in deeply. 'Why?'

It is as if he is prompting her. She is quick to take up the cue. 'Because you're my brother, my only real brother. Because if you don't give me shelter, no one will. Because the whole world knows you to be a man who protects the poor and friendless. Because you can plead for me before the king. Because you are Absalom. Because I love you.'

Absalom considers her reply for a long time, in silence, and finds it satisfactory. He does not speak. He simply extends his hand to her. Tamar bows to him. He has not disowned her. She is still his sister. The mob murmurs its approbation and excitement.

Throughout Absalom has looked only at her; from the way he has carried himself he might be alone with her in the street. Nothing, it seems, is easier for him than to see himself, without misgiving or reservation, as he is determined the watching crowd shall see him: as a man of ruth and power.

And of passion and pride, too. His bare arms are about her shoulders, the frown on his brow has contracted and deepened, he stands motionless, waiting for the full meaning of all she has told him to penetrate him, to strike root in him; and then to begin drawing him into itself. Drawing his anger and strength; his love for her and his ambitions for himself; all he has taken for granted in the past and will never be able to take for granted again. Even his beauty and the grace of his movements, without which he would not be Absalom, are drawn too, visibly altered by the ugliness that has been planted within him; not lessened, but made purer, more tense, sadder. His shoulders swell, he lifts his face from her hair, his lips move. We cannot hear what he is saying, we do not know why Tamar looks up suddenly in surprise, and then lowers her gaze and comes closer yet to him. Perhaps he is uttering words of encouragement to her, or endearments, or promises of revenge; perhaps he is praying for her; perhaps he is simply raving, repeating Amnon's name like a curse. Involuntarily we draw closer. Our eager, nervous shuffle forward does not escape Absalom. He at once raises his voice, though he still looks straight at Tamar and appears to direct his words only to her.

What he says is disconnected and riddling, made up of so many bursts of phrases delivered in a menacingly level tone; its logic is wholly that of his self-regard, which he believes to be identical with the regard we have for him. He cannot permit the injury Amnon has done to his sister, and hence to himself, to be thought of as anything less than an outrage, an act of sacrilege; he cannot admit before us that a miserable creature like Amnon has the power to injure him. A conflict impossible to resolve? But Absalom resolves it, after a fashion.

'No one can harm you, Tamar. You're the princess, my sister, we're one family, parts of one another, we can't hurt each other without hurting ourselves. . . . Amnon will learn just how badly he's hurt himself, you needn't worry about that. Leave it to me. I'll do whatever's necessary to be done. . . . If you were a beggar-woman I'd take care of you, so how could you think that I'd turn you away? My sister! And Amnon dared to do it to you! . . . You are right to have gone through the streets, showing yourself to anyone who wanted to look at you. It's Amnon you were showing them, not yourself. We cannot be shamed by him. But we can shame him. We can do more than that, too, and we will. . . . Now put it out of your mind, don't think about it any more. I'll remember it for you. I'm the only one who'll remember it: me and our brother, Amnon.'

For the first time Absalom addresses us directly. 'Do you hear?' he shouts angrily at us. 'I'm the only one who'll remember any of this. Clear off! All of you! At once! There's nothing more for you to stare at!'

He turns towards the gate of his house, Tamar following him. But we don't obey his command to disperse until his men close the gate behind the two of them, and advance on us. Then, promptly, we scatter.

A quite different group assembles in the throne-room for the regular session of the council, some hours later. The only member common to the two groups, I am sure, is myself. By now it seems that practically everyone in the court, with the exception of David himself, has heard of the catastrophe that has befallen his daughter. No one as yet has dared to speak to him of it.

My father, however, has already called me into his office, where, trembling with fear and curiosity, he has demanded of me that I tell him everything I know about this 'unbelievable rumour' (but he believes it, you bet he believes it) this 'heinous deed', this 'unparalleled infamy'. (If you think my father talks like a newspaper editorial, you are quite right; and consider what native talent the man has; he does so without ever having seen a newspaper in his life.) Wagging his fingers, plucking his beard, running his hand over his round, bald, slightly sweaty head, he has told me twenty times that . . . he *told* me so. He told me that Amnon was dangerous, that I would get into trouble through Amnon, that I would get *him* into trouble through Amnon. And now – look! His advice to me was to leave the court, at once; to go anywhere, as long as it was away from David's wrath. Perhaps later, when the whole thing had blown over, if it ever did, I would be able to come back, it wouldn't be held against me that I'd been Amnon's friend. (He'd *told* me so!) But I was in danger now, any friend of Amnon's was, it could mean my death if I was seen about the court. Yes, death, he wasn't exaggerating; possibly it could mean something worse.

And this was his reward for having given me the opportunity to enter the court, for having done so much to advance my career, for having advised me at every stage! Of course, I'd known better than to follow his advice. I'd felt myself free to make friends with a madman, a dangerous beast, a fellow you could see from a mile off was capable of absolutely anything. Now his career, Shimeah's, was probably in ruins; perhaps all he had to look forward to because of me was relegation and ignominy. As if he hadn't begged me, pleaded with me, *told* me. . . .

All this (forgive me for dwelling on the interview, but I have a certain fondness, as you must by now have guessed, for my craven papa) – all this interspersed with pop-eyed, wet-lipped, whispered questions about the unspeakable crime, the heinous deed, the unmentionable atrocity, itself. I mean, was it true that Amnon had actually – ? Or had he only tried . . . you know? For how long had he been planning to do it? Some people were saying that Tamar had really led him on, provoked him: did I know anything about that? What was the truth of the incomprehensible stories people were telling one another about the food and drink Amnon was supposed to have prepared for Tamar: had he been drunk, was it true that the food he'd given her had been drugged? Why had she gone to Absalom? Why had she walked about the streets of the city? Did Amnon know she'd gone to Absalom? And what if she was pregnant? Such things did happen. . . . Did I know if she was pregnant?

No, I did not know if she was pregnant. How could I? ('Of course,' my father promptly and apologetically agreed, to do him justice.) Naturally, I also denied knowing the answers to the rest of his questions. All I knew, I claimed, was what I'd heard in the palace that morning. I'd been as astonished as everyone else to hear of it. And if I seemed to take it less tragically than my father: after all, I pointed out, I'd never much cared for Tamar, and what had happened to her didn't seem to me the end of the world. It was, I said, 'just another – '

'Outrageous! How dare you!' my father interrupted, before I could finish the phrase. But he was too busy rolling his eyes about, suddenly fearing a spy in every corner, to put the right amount of moral fervour into his voice.

Anyway, I went on, it would be absurd for me to flee the court now. Why should I? Running away could only look like an admission of guilt; and I had no guilt to admit to. I was not Amnon's brother, I was not his father, still less (if that were possible) was I his sister, I wasn't responsible for his mad deeds.

My father listened to me gloomily; for the moment he had no more to say, perhaps because he felt the force of my argument. However, he did later give me a formal warning; from a man like him it could almost have been called a profession of faith.

'If you get into trouble,' he said, 'I'll disown you. I've got to look after myself. I warned you and you took no notice of what I said. So I'm going to make no move to help you. God alone knows if it will help me, but it's the least I can do for myself. Isn't that so? Isn't that fair?'

Extraordinary man that he was, he announced his intention – in case of need – to jettison all concern for me, to sever all ties between us; then he asked me in advance for moral approval of his action. What could I do but give it to him? Everybody is entitled to have his faith respected. Even my father.

The gloom into which his initial excitement had declined then sank even lower into a mood of stranded, hulk-like helplessness. 'What's the king going to do when he hears about it?' he asked, as if he were the very first man in the palace to raise the question. 'Who is going to tell him? What's going to become of us all?'

I had no inside information to offer him on these questions either. For the answers to them, he and I (and you) must go forward or back to where we were before the long filial digression or recollection I have just concluded. To the throne-room, that is; to the group I have left waiting in a frenzy of restrained anticipation for the arrival of the king.

Be assured, nothing has changed there during our absence. The king hasn't yet arrived. Judging from the look on his face and his manner of fingering the hilt of his sword, I would say that even the youngest officer on duty has heard of the scandal which is about to break, and is having vivid fantasies of being called upon to do more than ceremonial duties today: he sees himself making arrests, carrying out summary executions, pursuing fugitives. The rest of us are a little more restrained. None of us says a word of what is uppermost in our minds; but with many specious nods and wrinklings of our foreheads, much play with the corners of our mouths, meaningful movements of our eyes, twitches of our shoulders and flarings of our fingers, while we exchange our greetings and commonplaces about the weather, we signal to one another that we are fully in the know (heaven forbid, for the sake of our reputations as men of affairs, that we shouldn't be), and that we are deeply apprehensive of what is about to pass before us. Deeply commiserative too: that also goes without saying.

At last the king arrives. He looks as he did the last time we saw him here: small, bright, in command, his alertness tinctured to just the right degree with indifference, his

aloofness with fatigue. On his way to the throne he pauses
to greet some of the people who are stepping back and
bowing to him, and his enquiries after their welfare appear
all the more good-natured and considerate precisely because they are so perfunctory, those of a man with much
more important things on his mind. He takes his place on
the throne and smooths down his robes before the page on
duty can do it for him. The princes who are in the room
draw closer to him, their eyes enormous with their
unspoken news, their lips trembling with the effort to
contain it. Ira steps forward with a scroll in his hand, on
which is inscribed today's order of business. We sigh, but
not out of boredom. The king's entry has never seemed to
us so swift before; somehow so irrevocable. We are in for
it now, and so is he. Suddenly we find ourselves wishing
we were somewhere else.

Ira begins to read from the scroll. His voice quavers. Is
it his duty as chief minister, seeing that none of the
princes have spoken, to tell the king what has happened to
his daughter? There is nothing of the slightest importance
on the scroll; but the old man draws out the reading of it
interminably, partly because he wants to delay coming to
its end, partly because he can't help stumbling, losing his
place, staring down in blank silence at the document in his
hand. David is puzzled, but patient. Ira looks up, the
scroll drops from his hand, his face puckers, it seems to
strive towards an expression – an order – it cannot attain.
'My lord – ' he says hopelessly.

A movement at the door. Absalom enters. The whole
room knows it at once, even though he hardly comes
beyond the threshold. He looks across the room, above our
heads, straight at David. It is obvious to him that the king
knows nothing: if he did, he would not be where he is, and
nor would we.

Absalom waits before speaking. His voice is calm but resolute. He addresses the king directly.

'I have bad news for you.'

10

Love and hatred have grown together, they wear the same expression, they make demands that can never be fulfilled in order to justify their ancient rages. David has loved his children exorbitantly, gluttonously, with passions that have overwhelmed him and have yet been his instruments, abnegations that have swollen his pride, generosities that have crushed their recipients. What is he to do, now he has heard that the son to whom he gave so much of himself at their last meeting has violated the daughter he has always adored? Who is he to blame, now he has learned that in lavishing tenderness and prayer over Amnon he was blindly sending his daughter to her destruction?

He blames himself, of course. Amnon, as well. But he blames Tamar most of all.

How unjust, you want to cry out. (That's what many of us in the throne-room want to cry out, too.) You are right and so are we. But we know that David has not become king and ruler over us through a strict, undeviating regard for justice; his attachment to it has never been stronger than his attachment to himself, his career, his power, his political skills, his prestige. He has always been prepared to cut his losses; he has never allied himself to defeat. Least of all has he allied himself to his own defeats. Tamar has been ruined; he was tricked and fooled into contributing to her ruin; she is therefore doubly a source of discredit to him; he will have no more to do with her. The logic of his response is merciless and irresistible; and once he has adopted it, his love for her and his guilt – guilt for what he is doing now, guilt for what he did the night before – can only make his repudiation of her fiercer. He must see a premonition of disaster as the very deepest of the feelings he had always had about her. She had been beyond his keeping, his regard for her had always included an element of despair. So it is even possible for him to greet the news with cries of pain that sound strangely akin to those of relief: at least he knows now what it was he had so much dreaded in the past.

Yet you must not misunderstand me. David does not blame Tamar for having been ravished. He may be intolerably cunning and devious, he may grope unerringly through the darkness of his own soul towards the personal supremacy he cannot live without, but he isn't mad, he isn't a fool, he doesn't pretend that she could have led on Amnon, as some imbeciles around the palace have already shown themselves ready to believe. David doesn't need to follow their example. The disgrace she is in means less to him than the fact that – disgraced – she is not present, he hasn't seen her, she has become an abstraction to him; and by her own choice. She has turned away from him. It is for that that he blames her, and will never be able to forgive her. She has gone to Absalom.

To Absalom, who has given his own meaning, the king is sure, to her choice. To Absalom, who brings him bad news like a challenge; and then stands before him, declaring in every word and gesture, as David interprets them, that he is incapable of meeting the challenge.

David: 'And you come and yell out these things in my council chamber, in front of the whole court! Couldn't you think what they would mean to me? Couldn't you speak to me alone before telling the whole world?'

Absalom: 'There isn't a soul here who didn't know all about it before I spoke. Except for *you*.'

We quail, expecting David to look from the one to the other of us, accusing us in his glance of being cowards, liars, keepers of secrets from him. But he does not do it. Instead, he reads into what Absalom has said an implication we would never have dared to find.

'So I'm finished, am I? An old man whom no one bothers to keep informed? They must go to you, they must wait for you. Everyone must run to you, as Tamar has done.'

'You have said it, not me.'

Provoking the reactions which transform each previous misunderstanding into a truth, the two are able to use each other, turn and turn about, as stepping-stones towards the adoption of finally intransigent and irreconcilable positions. We all know how such a process works; we have all been actively involved in it at one time or another. What would any of our institutions, from marriage to diplomacy, be without it? We stand in the council chamber, we are wearing formal dress, we have gathered together to carry on important business of the state; nevertheless we are like children watching their parents quarrel over the dinner-table; like children we are frightened and fascinated by what we witness, foreseeing in it the destruction of our house and the overthrow of the security we have known. David and Absalom, father and son, princely politicians and leaders of men, bring to the task all the energy and misguided acumen at their command. Each cannot tell his own or the other's claims from denials, disavowals from accusations, affirmations from attacks. Even titles or appellations become a ground of conflict between them.

If Absalom calls Tamar 'my sister' he is disputing David's right to call her his daughter; if David calls her 'your sister' he is pretending that Absalom has wrested from him what he is anxious to surrender, or has already irresponsibly turned adrift, left with no protector but Absalom. When Absalom demands justice he is impudently trying to arrogate to himself the king's privilege of judging; when David reserves to himself that privilege then Absalom knows that justice will not be done, for justice belongs to no man, not even to the king, but to the community beyond him and greater than him, which the king must serve.

Inevitably, the angrier the king is with Absalom, the less inclined he is to turn his wrath against Amnon, if only because Absalom wants him to. And though Absalom speaks of the duties of the king, the authority of the state, the will of the people, the protection of the helpless, the judgement of posterity – such phrases come readily to Absalom's lips, even when he is as moved as he is now – it is to the single issue of the punishment of Amnon that David reduces all Absalom's invocations. In David's eyes Amnon is guilty, there is no question about it. But he will not say, he will not even hint, what penalty he will exact for the crime; or whether Amnon will have to suffer any penalty other than his father's displeasure.

Until Absalom, infuriated by the king's evasiveness, is driven for the first time to make explicit his ultimate demand. 'Amnon must be punished according to the law, like anyone else. "A man who uncovers his sister's naked-ness shall be cut off in the sight of the people": that's what the law lays down. I insist that the law be carried out. For my sister's sake I demand my brother's death.'

David leans back in his chair and answers quietly. 'So that you will have one less rival for my throne.'

At last that, too, has been said: it has been made plain what is at stake between them. Now we understand David's movement in the chair, before he spoke. He is challenging Absalom to oust him from it, if he can.

Absalom cries out: 'Think what you are saying!' David does not answer, and Absalom plunges forward to meet the charge. 'Amnon will never sit in your throne. I will see to it.'

'Exactly.'

'And how much longer will you occupy the throne if you refuse to carry out the law? Think what you are doing! If the king isn't bound by the law, then who is? Why should anyone in this room obey the law, if he sees that it means nothing to the king? Why should you have the power to jail a thief or hang a traitor? Who is the traitor when the king betrays the laws – the king, or the man who overthrows him? Don't you understand, there can be no end to what you're beginning. You leave us no alternative.'

'To what?'

Absalom isn't afraid to say the words: 'Rebellion. Upheaval.'

Nor is the king upset by them. 'And all out of your love of law and order?'

'No, out of my love for justice, which is more important to me than either.'

Absalom's arguments are the stronger; we cannot doubt it. Yet his position appears to become weaker and weaker, the longer the dispute between them continues. Not only because he is appealing for harshness while David, whatever his reasons may be, is on the side of clemency; nor because David has made suspect Absalom's motives in demanding Amnon's death; nor even because David has the power, with a beck of the head, to have Absalom arrested for seditious talk, so that the clemency he is objecting to when applied to another is helping him too. All these demonstrate but do not define David's readiness to follow his own judgement, no matter how perverse or cruel it may be, as to what will best serve him; his confidence in his right to be moved or not, as he pleases, by the logical strength of an argument, or by the threatening tone in which it is couched, or by the expectations which others have of him, or by the commitments of his own past.

But what has such a display of self-will to do with justice? With the rights and wrongs of the debate between them? To Absalom, nothing. To David, everything. Which is in itself another way of describing David's power. He knows that unreason and fatality have always been among the forces through which he has worked and which have worked upon him, and he accepts that it should be so; Absalom does not. Therefore, it is Absalom who appears vain, shallow, self-obsessed, bloodthirsty, bemused by abstractions; while David, in his unmoving ivory throne, rides upon the very crest of that tidal equipoise between the violence of law and the violence of lawlessness, which we call peace and sovereignty. It is faith, not expediency, which is David's last resource: faith in the power which has given him his power. He prays to it, he governs his polity by it, he knows the order and anarchy of the universe to depend upon it.

But I've already used too many words to describe something that is plain to the simplest person in the room. Absalom is not the simplest person in the room (let me, looking around at the assembled courtiers, charitably grant him that much); nevertheless, he chooses to take that exacting role upon himself. He appeals to his brothers to help him make the king do his duty; he warns them that if Amnon's crime goes unpunished then they too will be in danger, for Amnon will feel himself free to commit any crime imaginable against any of the king's children; he reminds them of the disrespect the family will fall into if it becomes known abroad not only that such a crime has been committed, but that it has had no consequences, been treated as a trifle.

'You think our neighbours are in any position to disapprove? With their habits?' David puts in sardonically at that point. He has sunk farther into his chair, and protruded his head a little, lizard-like both in his posture and in the unblinking silence of the gaze he has fixed on Absalom.

Absalom's arguments are valid and unavailing. His brothers, who had waited for him to break the news to the king, as if he were indeed their leader, and had dared to cry out only after he had spoken – those brothers of his now simply don't want to listen to him. Some of them gesture to him surreptitiously, others actually interrupt him. They want him to shut up, to leave it alone. This isn't the time or the place for what he is saying; he isn't helping anyone; let them consider it all later or in private; let the whole unhappy meeting come to its end.

'I would never, never have believed it,' Absalom finally exclaims. 'That I'd have to plead that a man who did such a thing to our sister should get the punishment he deserves – !'

He looks about him, and what he sees in our faces discourages and baffles him further. Only the thought of Tamar herself gives him the strength to turn once more to the king and say his last words to him. 'Tamar will learn what's happened here this morning. She is my sister, and a princess, and she will know how to behave towards a father who treats her as you have.'

125

David is silent; for a moment unable to move. Then he rouses himself. To Ira's surprise, to the surprise of us all, he calls the chancellor.

'You hadn't finished. There are matters that must be attended to. We have work to do.'

Who can tell how much it may have cost him to give that order; and then to sit on the throne, listening, nodding his head occasionally, speaking when he has to, while the tedious affairs of the day are dispatched. Still, he does it; and what's more, he does it in a manner which suggests that he is making the effort as much for Absalom's sake as for his own. He is trying to save him from further humiliation and self-exposure; he is giving him time to recover.

Absalom is not grateful for the respite. But it's unheard-of for anyone to leave the throne-room before the king, and for all his talk of rebellion just a few minutes previously, he cannot bring himself to break the tradition. Instead, he stands with his arms folded and a look of contempt and outrage on his face, waiting for the moment of release.

David will not give it to him. On his way out of the room he stops in front of Absalom. For the onlooker, certainly for David himself, there is pathos in the disparity in height between them; in the difficulty he has in putting his hand on his son's shoulder.

'Absalom,' he says, issuing the order in a suddenly tremulous, beseeching voice, 'you will dine with me. We will talk of other things. There are other subjects we can talk about.'

The day continues. The same day still, is it? It must be. I can hardly remember when it began; I have had no sleep; it seems years have passed since I was last alone with Amnon in his house.

We had drunk wine, I recall, the memory coming to me as if from another world; we had quarrelled; later on we had talked; then Tamar had arrived. Nothing had yet happened that would need to be remembered by any of us; nothing that would cause us to be remembered by others. Then, when all had been anticipation, not deed, there had still been a chance of the day being assumed into that eternity of the nondescript which is perhaps the truest eternity we shall ever attain; the moments when history is made or fame secured being no more than intrusions and interruptions into eternity, fractures of it, and never, as we like to suppose, its fulfilment among us. Not for the first time it occurs to me that we are most closely bound to eternity when we carry out those actions to which we attach least importance: when we yawn, or scratch ourselves, or blink in a sudden blaze of sunlight, or take out our cocks and have the satisfaction of peeing against a wall, or listen absently to the conversation of bores. For then we are truly indistinguishable from one another; your nervous system is as mine; there is neither succession nor precession; only our shared, timeless commonalty.

Today, as on any other, I yawn, scratch myself, piss, I blink in the sunlight when I come out of the palace. But I also make my way to Amnon's house, to see what he is doing and to hear what he has to say. I have to. The day, that has already gone on for so long, is not like any other. It is set apart; and so are those of us who have allowed ourselves to be caught within it. For the first time I have a vivid intimation of what that might mean. For the first time, with a mixture of sick apprehension and excitement, I see myself here, always here, always before you, condemned to remember, explain, present and comment upon actions I cannot change; banished from the ordinary oblivion to which I had once, not long before, been entitled.

I find Amnon to be depressed. He is also exhausted, naturally enough, after such a night. (Even I, who – shall I say? – exerted myself so much less than he, am feeling oddly detached and weightless for lack of sleep; only my itchy eyes seem definitely to belong to me.) Before coming to the house I expected to hear abuse and reproaches, ravings against myself and Tamar. I was wrong.

He is so depressed he can hardly open his mouth. He is fully clothed, but he shows no sign of being about to go out; indeed, he doesn't stir from the chair in which he sits, his legs splayed out in front of him, his hands hanging down between them, his chin either sunk against his chest or pointing towards the ceiling, apparently unable to hold any position between. His greeting had been a single sideways slide of his eyes; a shake of his head his answer to my hearty enquiry how he was feeling; total immobility his response to my innocent wonder if his night with Tamar had 'come up to expectations'. (I'd chosen the phrase with some care, on my way to his house from the palace.)

We sit together without speaking for some time. Amnon appears to fall asleep, twitches suddenly with his feet and shoulders, and is awake again. At least I see his black eyelashes flickering.

'So what happened?' I demand finally, like the bluff, forthright friend whose tones I have decided it would be best for me to adopt.

Amnon doesn't answer at once. But it is not because he

is weighing his words so scrupulously. His chin tilted ceilingward, he says 'Nothing.'

'Nothing? What do you mean?'

But he merely repeats the word. 'Nothing.'

'You mean you just let her go?'

'No.'

'Then what did you do?'

'Nothing.'

'That's not what Tamar's telling everyone.'

Even this irritated warning of mine, which I hadn't intended uttering quite so soon, has little effect on Amnon. 'Then you know what happened,' he merely says. 'Why do you bother me about it?'

'It's true, then, is it?'

'You should know.'

I look sharply at him. But what I see reassures me. He isn't hinting that he has guessed where I spent the night: he is simply letting me know that he doesn't care what Tamar is saying about him, and what I or anyone else make of it.

I try again. 'Tamar went to Absalom. She didn't go back to the palace. Absalom told the king about it. Everyone knows by now; the whole city.'

'I thought I heard more people than usual in the street outside,' Amnon remarks indifferently. 'They must be waiting for something to happen.'

'They are. I had to push my way through them to get here.'

His head sinks down, his lips pout further forward, he rubs his hands vaguely together, and then desists, as if even that effort is too much for him.

'What are you going to do?' I ask.

'About the people outside?'

'No, of course not. About Tamar. About David. About

Absalom. About the whole business. You've got to do something.'

'Why?'

'Well, you were certainly energetic enough in getting yourself into trouble, weren't you?'

'I know. That was the mistake I made. Look,' he adds, surprising me with the sudden vigour of his tone, 'I'm sorry for Tamar. I'm sorry I ever hurt her. I was mad. I see it now. But she's mad, too, to think it matters. It doesn't. We make up rules, and then we make up emotions to go with them. It's nonsense. If we had other rules we'd have the same emotions about different things. That's all there is to it.'

Amnon, the philosopher. Amnon, the quietist. Amnon, the stoic acceptor of the miseries he's inflicted on others. It's enough to turn one's stomach. However, I take him up on it mildly enough.

'If we're going to have the emotions anyway, then perhaps that's precisely why they do matter. Why they must matter.'

His vigour has left him as abruptly as it came. 'You think so?' he asks, without curiosity.

'What else is there?'

'Nothing. Death.'

One of the things that most irritates me about our exchange is that I don't have to come to Amnon in order to ask such questions and to hear such replies: I could always stay at home and commune with myself for five minutes. Yet his last words have made me suddenly vigilant. Coiled motionlessly within my impatience, like the vivid, immaculate twist of colour inside a glass marble, is the answer to a problem which has been worrying me for longer than I have suspected. After all, I have just come from a room where I have heard death, his death, being treated as a possibility, a matter of choice. And now he too has spoken of it. To me: who else? Looking at Amnon, with his sandalled feet and hanging hands, I feel I have never been closer to him or more detached from him; he has ceased to be human and has already become no more than a rock-face confronting me, a tree, a body of water, an object, any natural phenomenon which I can examine but which cannot examine me. I am unable to withdraw. I have interfered so much, used the only kind of power I have to such effect, I must now continue to the end. There can be no end other than the one he has just named.

Call me an artist, if you like. I won't take it as a compliment. Any more than I will take it as an insult if you call me a pathologically malicious busybody who is compelled to make up for his own emotional vacuity by manipulating the passions and lives of others. Either way, I have to see my *oeuvre* completed, given its inevitable, final shape; the shape for which Amnon, Tamar and Absalom are themselves seeking, though it eludes each of them on his own.

How penurious our imaginations are! How limited our ingenuities! There is no need for me to talk of Osiris and Isis, of Baal and Anat, of Tammuz and Innana-Ishtar: brothers and sisters, lovers in their season, explorers of the underworld of darkness and disintegration. I'd do just as well to speak to you of a wolf that lay in bed and pretended to be sick, like Amnon, until there came to him a pretty virgin with a gift of food, like Tamar. Then the wolf sprang on Little Red Riding Hood and devoured her.

Now the wolf must die. The wolf himself says so. The wolf says there is nothing else. The wolf is looking for his death. Absalom, woodman, shepherd, rebellious son, you can sharpen your axe.

11

Actually, the blade Absalom was sharpening was intended in the first place for my own throat. I hadn't gone more than fifty yards from Amnon's house before I was seized by a group of Absalom's toughs who carried me to their boss. Once he had me in his hands Absalom told me he wanted 'the truth. The whole story. Everything.' Then he put a knife against my throat.

The edge of it was hard against my skin; more coarse than sharp, but painful enough. Absalom held the knife in one hand; he had a fistful of my hair in the other, and pulled my head back to expose my neck. From beneath, his face looked like something in a nonsensical dream: his red lower lip overhung a raging beard; his nose protruded above, each nostril shaped exactly like the sole of a tiny foot.

'No,' he said. 'I don't think I'll kill you.' The gleam of the knife passed across my vision, then his fist went into my eye, the blade pressed against my ear. 'I'll cut your ears off, that's what I'll do. I'll slit your nose. I'll put your eyes out. Then I'll send you home to your father.'

The hoodlums who had dragged me to the house uttered a sound of mirth and impatience: their kind of laugh. I couldn't see them. Behind Absalom's head there was only the cool, white ceiling, immeasureably distant from me. My head was yanked further back. Though my hands weren't bound, I was too frightened to bring them up to try to fend him off, or even to help me keep my balance. A final yank, my legs shot away from under me, and I was on the floor. One of Absalom's feet rose in the air and came enquiringly towards me, like the muzzle of a dog; then it flew forward, catching me under the chin. Another foot landed in my ribs. I was attacked from all sides, by everyone in the room; they shouted, cursed, laughed, egged each other on, while I rolled about trying to protect my face and my genitals. The violence of the blows was incredible. I mean that in the strictest sense: I could not believe in them, even while they were falling, my nerves couldn't tell what they were, these forces or explosions that burst outside me, struck inwards with a hideous, rupturing intimacy, transformed themselves into whirling lights and intolerable textures my innermost senses had to crawl over. I ached for weeks afterwards, I had to spend days in bed, recovering from the bruises and shock of the attack. And I was grateful to do it; I felt I'd got off lightly. For Absalom had not been joking, of that I was sure.

Yet he wasn't serious either. This did nothing to lessen the danger I was in. It's a great delusion to suppose that serious deeds (like murder) are the consequence only of serious emotions or intentions. Not at all. People who don't know what they feel are quite capable of committing murder – or suicide, for that matter – in order to prove how serious and determined they are. It happens all the time. It could have happened to me, that afternoon.

It didn't, though, as you know. After a while (I have no idea how long) Absalom told his boys to lay off, and they obeyed him. I was prostrate on the floor, hardly aware that the attack had stopped. The air I gasped for was outside me; it had become flat and hard, like cardboard; I couldn't fit it into my lungs. Absalom walked to and fro, threatening me with unspeakable things if I didn't tell him – wouldn't co-operate – tried to fob him off. . . . Everybody knew Amnon and I – I was always in and out of his house. . . . So I'd better – he'd be satisfied only if. . . .

I'm not sure if his sentences and threats really were left unfinished or whether they only seemed so because my consciousness lapsed away from me and came back as if after long, utterly featureless journeys. Someone fetched a jug of water and poured it over my head. Someone dragged me outside, into a bathroom, where I began to whoop and heave convulsively. Nausea was hot inside me, everywhere at once; it constricted my head, it ran down my legs. After more heaving I threw up some blackish stuff in which were mixed a few elastic white fragments, with filaments attaching them to the rest, like stars viewed through half-closed eyes, or plasm in a web. I stared at the fragments with all the owlish intensity, it now occurs to me, of one of your pot-smoking poets; bemusedly convinced, as they with their spewings, that the sight would be enormously meaningful if only I could get over the difficulty of ascribing a meaning to it. I was dragged back into the room. Nausea had receded; now it was pain's turn once more.

'You'll speak all right.' Those were the first words I heard from Absalom on my return; he might have been saying nothing else all the time I had been out of the room. 'You'll tell me the lot. You won't dare do anything else.'

'Of course,' I yelled.

At these words rills of tears and blood ran disgustingly back into my nose and mouth, instead of out of them. But I managed to go on. 'What's there you don't know already? For God's sake, what more do you want to learn?'

The answer, I found out, was a great deal. His unsuccessful meeting with his father had infuriated

Absalom: it had left him at a loss, even afraid. He wanted to reach out at Amnon, but did not dare to do so; he had grabbed at me instead; he wanted to watch me squirm; he wanted to extort something from me – a self-inculpation, an apology, an explanation – that would set him upon a path from which he need never turn back. He wanted help or guidance, I could almost say; though in the circumstances, and from a man like Absalom, such an appeal could take the form only of threats and knocks intended to give the impression that he was already grimly and irrevocably determined on a course of action.

Anyway, I was ready to oblige. An hour later, I was seated in a comfortable chair; ointment had been put on my cuts and a cold cloth was pressed against the swelling that had risen on my cheekbone; I was no longer in the bare, closed-off cell at the back of the house which the ambitious Absalom apparently made use of as a private prison and interrogation chamber, but sat in one of his elegant living-rooms. Even in the state I was in I could see that Absalom's house, which I had never before entered, was like a little court, a small palace. Everything in it, from the furniture in the room to the traffic in the corridors outside, indicated that its master was a man with wives, friends, followers, a place in society. Not to mention his own gang of goons. The contrast between this house and Amnon's neurotic bachelor establishment was extreme.

Indeed, on the lap of the master of the house, as he sat opposite me, was a barefoot child, no more than about a year old, who had somehow escaped from her nursemaid and come crawling on her own into the room. Absalom had at once snatched her up, like a devoted papa; while we talked he absently stroked the baby's naked legs, or lowered his lips to the gleaming hair that stood up in wisps about her head. From deep within her own infant eternity of being, the baby studied me. Never used yet for walking, her legs tapered down to feet and ankles as soft and round as mushrooms, which Absalom's hands were big enough to cup together in a single, gentle grasp. Only an hour before he had been torturing me; now, for my benefit as much as the infant's, I suspect, I had to watch him kissing and fondling as well.

I remain in that chair: that day, days that follow it. Absalom sits opposite me. His expression is morose. He does not trust me. I puzzle him. I disgust him. He considers me a traitor by profession and a reactionary by inclination; in his more charitable moods he chooses to look upon me as nothing more than a frivolous chatterbox, the typical product of a corrupt court and an outmoded social system. I don't mind: personally, I mean. I wouldn't mind at all if the consequence were not that he never opens up to me, he never really tells me what he is thinking.

Yet he appears to listen to me. Even more: he appears to do what I suggest. He never rewards me with an acknowledgement that my ideas are the right ones, in the circumstances; still less do I ever get an expression of gratitude from him. He stares at me, he grunts, he dismisses me with a nod of his big, stupid, handsome head. Then he goes to the court and works hard for his father, like a dutiful son, like the conscientious counsellor and civil servant I have advised him to become. I have told him to become a member of as many of the important political and economic committees as he can; and he has done so. I have urged him to try and pack the committees he serves on with people in the court or outside it whom he knows to be his supporters, or of people whom he thinks will become his supporters if he favours them; and he has done his best to bring such a state of affairs about. I have advised him to cultivate assiduously the friendship of his brothers – all but one of them; and he has done that too. He has taken pains to establish cordial relations with the ambassadors of our near and more distant neighbours; he travels more widely about the country than before; he sees to it that his many deeds of charity receive more publicity, one way and another, than in the past: all according to my prescriptions. He has, also on my advice, abandoned the scheme he once had of putting his body-guard into a distinctive apparel.

Restraint, an absence of haste in all things, and, above all, much hard work: these are what I have counselled Absalom. Too much is at stake, I have told him, for him to indulge himself in ill-considered action. A premature move and his entire future – that consecrated, glittering, articulated prospect, where all will be in measure and he will be the measure of all – will be lost to him and to the country. But if he plays his hand correctly, then the punishment of Amnon can be far more than the occasion when revenge is taken, when an account is settled: it can be the moment for Absalom, effectively, to assert his power within the family, the court, and the state as a whole.

'Then people will say I did it only in order to get rid of a rival,' Absalom objects, repeating the accusation his father has already made against him.

'Well, you will have got rid of a rival,' I answer.

We have had that particular exchange, in just those words, again and again: I don't know how many times. Each time Absalom speaks as if what he is saying has never been said before. Is it stupidity or policy on his part? Possibly both: stupid policy. It is perhaps his way of displaying his contempt for me. It isn't the only exchange of its kind, either. Far from it.

'If you're double-crossing Amnon like this, how do I know you aren't double-crossing me?' Thus Absalom, repeatedly. And I:

'You can't know. You can only trust your own judgement.'

Weeks, even months, pass. The summer is over. We might be caught in a dream, one of those dull yet obscurely menacing dreams that recur (or seem, even while you're having the dream, to be a recurrence of one you have had before). A fire burns in a grate at the far end of the room, but the chill strikes upwards from the paved floor. Absalom strokes his hair back, lovingly following the curve of it over his own skull, and down the back of his neck. Yet again he repeats a stale accusation against me.

'You just want to delay things in the hope that I'll lose my interest in the whole affair.'

I reply as I always do, making the same noises as before: my story has always been that I am helping Absalom because of my moral outrage at Amnon's crime. The words serve well enough. Almost any words would.

The truth, all considerations of policy aside, is that Absalom himself is caught up in the languor of anticipation. His inertia is almost like that of a lover with his mistress naked in his arms, an undisturbed night ahead of them, the swoon of expectancy so completely over him that he is already contented, unwilling to lose what he has for the sake of what he has to get. Amnon will never be more in Absalom's power than he is now, while Absalom plans and delays his death, and Amnon is ignorant of it.

Therefore, Absalom needs me. Not so much for the

advice I give him so freely and which he follows so ungraciously. He needs me to be his spy on Amnon, his eye, his ear, his arm around Amnon, the one who brings him the news of what Amnon says, where he goes, who he is seeing, what he eats, what he drinks, how much he drinks. Without me his anticipation would be incomplete, defective; he could never have the sensation, which so much delights him, of keeping his unconscious victim continually under his scrutiny and in his control. Huntsman, hawk, subtle schemer, slow ripener of vengeance, man of secret power: for all these roles the presence of Amnon's best friend, in the chair opposite him, is essential to Absalom.

Hence the liberties I take, the fact that I am not afraid to tease Absalom, to give him ambiguous answers, to proffer my advice to him as if he, and not Amnon, were my best friend. Besides, however suspicious of me Absalom might sometimes be, it is really beyond his powers to be surprised that I should have chosen to work for him. Who wouldn't, in Absalom's opinion, jump at the opportunity to have a master like himself?

'You really believe,' Absalom says, repeating yet again one of my earliest brainwaves, 'you really believe that the king encouraged Amnon? That he told him he'd look after him, no matter what he did?'

How easy it is to flatter these princes, these plotters, these jockeys for power – and to make them feel insecure at the same time! Absalom's face had become wonderfully animated the first time I suggested that the king had been behind Amnon's assault on Tamar, which had always really, secretly, viciously, been directed against Absalom himself. It flatters his vanity to believe this, it justifies in advance anything he may do in retaliation, it makes him feel he is constantly in danger.

'It's difficult to think of any other reason for the king's behaviour,' I reply, as Absalom wishes me to do, as I have replied so many times before.

Such visits to Absalom's house all take place at night. I am invariably met at the door by the same porter, a decorative, kilted, taciturn black from Nubia or somewhere farther south, who leads me through the house into a small antechamber, where I wait until Absalom opens an inner door and lets me into the room behind. I have the strong impression that I am not the only visitor to the house who arrives thus; is escorted to this chamber; who waits in the same manner.

I have tried consistently, as you may well suppose, to see more of Absalom's house and the people in it than he would wish me to. By dint of much effort and a little money I have got the porter to let me in early for my appointments, to allow me to dawdle behind him on the way to the antechamber, to leave its door ajar so that I can see into the next courtyard. I make the most of these exiguous opportunities; but I can't say that my enterprise has been greatly rewarded. No revelations. I do sometimes see faces from the court which surprise me; for the rest his visitors are not of any particular interest. Beggars, kinsmen of his mother's from Geshur, itinerant preachers and poets looking for a patron, a variety of travelling salesmen, the inevitable proportion of outright madmen that any eminent public figure attracts. . . . Frankly, I had hoped for more.

However, I have managed to see more than I would otherwise have done of the members of Absalom's bodyguard: my kidnapping acquaintances, the ones whose task it will be to kill Amnon when the time finally comes.

They are young; they have a disaffected, middle-class look about them; they plainly consider themselves to be the members of an *élite* of some sort. Of tomorrow's sort; if their boss's plans turn out well. When they aren't just sitting about, or skylarking with the women servants, or eating and drinking, or gambling, they keep in trim by fighting among themselves: they are always wrestling together like puppies, practising with their swords, going at one another with staves. Though they do not wear a uniform they have all adopted the same style of wearing their hair – cropped short, with a straight fringe falling over their foreheads – and their beards too are kept short, and cut square at the corners. It is difficult to tell them apart from one another: they could be brothers, or followers of a special cult.

What most surprises me about these blackguards, seeing them week after week, is their patience. They live for violence, presumably: for the self-forgetfulness of action, for the stillness and sharpness of those moments which precede great danger, for the satiated fatigue which follows it. But how much idleness they have to put up with; how much waiting between times! I would never be able to endure it.

Well, I hope they all come to the sticky ends they are looking for. Believe me, I have as much pity for them as they would have for me, if Absalom were to point in my direction, too, after giving them the signal to finish off Amnon. Which is precisely what I suspect Absalom of intending to do.

The inner door opened; I turned, expecting to see Absalom; I saw Tamar.

An early visit of mine to the house or a late one: I

cannot tell, it is of no consequence. I turned, and Tamar was there. I turned, and she took a pace forward.

Tamar! She had become a victim, a scandal, a memory: not a girl I expected to meet. She was dressed like a widow; her hair was covered and so were her arms.

She did not greet me. Her eyes merely flickered when she saw me. I stared at her. So changed, and so little changed! Then changed again: for I remembered how I had seen her naked, stretched, flexed, ravaged; her secret declivities exposed in their hairy strength, their tender-rimmed vulnerability. She took another step forward. Only a few feet separated us. An unformed impulse beat up within me, and mounted higher still: I didn't know whether I wanted to strike her, or to beg her forgiveness, or to ask her to marry me; perhaps to do all of these. But even wilder yet was the hope that she had sought me out, for a purpose I could not guess at.

She was the first to break the silence between us.

'You are Absalom's friend now, I see.'

She spoke as before, holding her head still, her voice as indifferent to me as it had ever been.

'Yes.'

She nodded, and walked across the room to the door.

She was going. She had nothing to say to me. I wanted to call out, but I could not. Not a word, not a sound, there wasn't even a gesture I could make.

It's worthless, the power you acquire over others by betraying them! If you do it well enough, your victims don't even know that they are your victims. So they escape you. They close the door in your face, as Tamar did, leaving me standing alone in the room.

12

Remember, you have the advantage, as I do, of being in the know about the real nature of Absalom's intentions. Others in the court, less fortunate than you, who were still looking for drama and diversion out of our principals during this time had to make what they could out of his persistent refusal to acknowledge Amnon's existence in any way whatsoever. Such excitements. . . . Imagine, Absalom had sat through an entire meal at Amnon's side without addressing a word to him or even passing him a bowl! Would you believe it, he'd left out Amnon's name in reading to the king a list of the duties assigned to each of the princes, and then pretended not to hear when the king pointed out the omission to him! He'd marched straight at Amnon in a narrow passage, leaving it to Amnon to flatten himself against the wall at the last moment!

The biggest treats for such people were Amnon's repeated attempts to bring about a public reconciliation between himself and his brother. Every greeting, every proffered embrace, every speech appealing for forgiveness and friendship was rebuffed decisively. Wonderful! Each time Absalom remained silent and unyielding; he stared through Amnon or past him, or turned his back on him indifferently. Whereupon, as the mood might take him, Amnon sometimes cried big tears, or made half-hearted, threatening gestures behind Absalom's back, or struck himself on his chest and proclaimed, 'It serves me right. I don't deserve anything better. That's how everyone should treat me.'

Poor old Amnon. Does it serve him right? Is that how everyone should treat him?

Honestly, I can't help feeling sorry for him, when I see him at the palace (which I do rarely enough, for he seldom goes there), or at home, or in the street, or in the few houses he still visits. It's always the same tedious story. He's always thanking people for being so kind to him. He's always apologising and making excuses for social lapses which he imagines he is guilty of perpetrating. His eyes are always ready to fill with tears, especially when he is in his father's presence.

It doesn't matter. His emotions are shallow, labile, unconvincing even to himself. Nothing is of real importance to him. Bereft of purpose and passion, unable to take himself seriously as a contender for any of the prizes for which he once strove, devoid of a belief in his capacity to change either himself or the world, denied even the assuagements of a thoroughgoing guilt – Amnon is utterly, abjectly bored.

In my own fashion I can claim to be something of an expert on the subject. I've also explored the recesses of boredom, its toils, its secret temptations and luxuries, its extraordinary way of anticipating you, as it were, so that it seems to get at any possible object of your attention before you do. Because you are bored, you lose your power of concentration: then how bored you are, in turn, because you have lost that power! The mind jumps, flicks, whirrs, it skids about the surface of things like a drop of water on a heated metal plate; it is severed from the emotions which should give it depth, and the emotions are severed from what gives them persistence and continuity with one another. You are bored. Amnon is bored.

It can be seen even in the restless movements of his eyes,

in the habit he has developed of suddenly heaving his chest for breath in the midst of other people's talk. He lies late in his bed in the mornings; he spends hours fondling the ears of his dogs; he declines to take on commissions which his father offers him (it bores him to think about them, therefore he has so much more free time in which to be bored); he collects writings on a wide range of topics which he never reads; he sets out to visit friends, then has second thoughts and goes home again.

And he drinks. His breath almost always smells of wine. He has become what I think of as a soft drunk. That is, his drinking isn't noisy, it isn't boastful or dangerous to others, it appears to be without fury or purpose; usually it leads to nothing more than somnolence and perhaps a few tears, furtive or ostentatious as the case may be. As a result of too much booze and too little exercise he looks slack and heavy. There are veins in his eyes that shouldn't show there; the pout of his lips has become as gross and convoluted as a flower; his complexion is patchy, splotchy, yellow and grey as well as red. When he sits it is on the base of his spine; his walk is a slouch; the effort he has to make to keep himself upright is almost too much for him.

He is so bored, poor man, that sometimes I am tempted to lean over to him, and say in a confidential, reassuring manner, 'It's all right, Amnon. You haven't got long to put up with it all. Absalom is going to kill you soon enough.' Were I to do so, I conjecture, Amnon's eyes would at once fill with tears, or he might cry out in fear or rage; five minutes later he would be picking his nose and staring out of the window. Or putting down another drink.

Of course, I never do utter such a warning. I just watch him. Not for a moment would I want to deny to you that I have found myself sharing Absalom's lethargy, his fascinated brooding over the vengeance to come, his curiosity about how the ignorant victim lives while he can. Having seen Amnon lunge at an obscure life beyond life, I now have the privilege of accompanying him towards that death beyond which (except on so dubious an occasion as this) there is nothing. Nothing. When I am in Amnon's company the knowledge I have, and that Amnon does not have, never really leaves me. It tingles in my fingers; it strikes at my diaphragm; it constricts my breathing; it makes me dizzy, as if I have stood up too quickly after stooping; it is like the thought of money in the bank, or an illicit love affair; it makes me want to giggle.

So that's how it is, I tell myself again and again, to be a man under sentence of death! (I know, we are all under sentence of death. Do you suppose that diminishes my interest in him, for heaven's sake?) I can't say that it is an edifying spectacle. Through the invisible screen of my foreknowledge I see how time fidgets with him, how existence irritates him, what a burden his own mass has become. I try to imagine darkness invading every coil and vortex of his brain, stillness sinking through his limbs, the tongue of silence swollen fast in his mouth; later mouth, limbs and brain themselves undone, released from form, combined into forms that will know as little of Amnon as he of them.

In the meantime he waits, without realising for what he waits, or why. It is not edifying, as I've said, to see him; but it is engrossing. He is about to undergo that change which can be compared to no other.

Look. He blinks. He pulls at the lobe of his ear. He clears his throat and speaks.

No, he doesn't. At the last moment he thinks better of it. He closes his mouth before he has uttered a word, and waits with a bowed head for his father to carry on talking about some subject in which Amnon is plainly not interested. David, who has paused for Amnon's comment like an anxious don at a seminar, sees that the comment isn't going to be forthcoming, and finishes what he had begun to say. Then he asks Amnon to tell him frankly if he thinks the right decision has been taken.

'I'm sure it has, father,' Amnon answers humbly. 'You're always right.'

'Not always,' David answers.

Perhaps the strangest thing about exchanges of this kind, which have become very common between them, is that they both mean what they say. You can tell that by the dejected air with which they speak.

We are all stuck in the consequences of our actions, no mistake about it; David as much as the rest of us. He is stuck as Amnon's protector-in-chief, sympathiser-in-special, and forgiver-extraordinary. So when Amnon makes as if to go, David detains him. He enquires solicitously after Amnon's welfare. Amnon's replies are intended solely to please. He is fine, he assures David. Everything is fine. He has no complaints. No, he isn't hungry. He's sure he isn't hungry. He had an excellent breakfast before coming to the palace.

Another minute, and Amnon will be sniffing. Often enough, David joins him with a sniff or two.

Tamar is never mentioned by name between them. (Or, for that matter, by either of them when they are apart from one another.) However, David does frequently speak to Amnon of 'the misfortune that has befallen me', 'the grief of my age', 'the sorrow I've had to live through', and so forth. At any such utterance Amnon's head at once begins to sink lower, and a look of what I can only call patient shame comes upon his face.

'How could I expect,' David suddenly exclaims on this or another occasion, indeed on many occasions, 'that my children would not have learned from me how to do evil? How could I imagine that my crimes would be forgotten? When I look at you, Amnon – when I think of what you have done – then I see that God has used you to remind me of all I most regret in my life. Yet how cunning he is! How subtle are his punishments! He waits until I begin to flatter myself that I'm a changed man, another person – gentler, wiser, more considerate, less devoted to my own pleasures. Then he moves against me; then he strikes; then he shows me, in your actions, just what I have always been. It is as if he says to me, "David, do you want to see what your lusts look like? Do you want to know how obsession walks, how deceit breathes, what kind of a face appetite has? Then look at your first-born son! Look what he has done and to whom he has done it!" And I look at you, Amnon, and see the truth about myself that I can never alter.

'There is nothing that my children won't do. I know it. Where are they different from the sons of any other man? What they can imagine – they must try. Because they have so much – they sicken for what they lack. Where their hands can reach – they will put them. Before they die – they must see how it is to wound and kill. And I am no better; I am worse; I am their father and their king, and they are not mine. So let David suffer, he deserves it. Let David's children suffer, and curse their father. Let David go to his grave in wretchedness; it is time he was there. Let him try to use what life he still has only to think about the mystery and wonder of God, who for his purposes, not ours, created us along with rats and flies; who remembers all, forgives nothing, and is never deceived. Every mark on the world – let us never forget it – is marked for ever upon him.'

Well (to continue in his idiom for a moment), let the king go on in this manner. No one can stop him, anyway. He is the king. While he says such things, let him shed tears, kiss Amnon, and hug any other of his sons who may happen to be within reach. It's impossible not to be moved by the old man's grief and remorse. Impossible, too, not to be struck by the amazing absence of reproach with which he calls Amnon a criminal, the destroyer of his hopes, the blackener of his last years. To judge from his manner nothing could be less to the point between himself and Amnon, where they now stand, than recrimination and hostility.

But notice, please do notice, how David's outpourings have the effect of turning Amnon into little more than the unresisting instrument of God's wrath for the punishment of David; how Amnon's passions have become merely a version or reflection of David's; how David remains, in the midst of his contrition, the real boss of Israel and the man upon whom God's mighty interest is all but exclusively concentrated. I need hardly ask you to notice, again, that the sufferings of Tamar remain entirely unmentioned by either of these penitents.

But when, alone with Amnon, I hint delicately that such criticisms could be made of his father's declarations, Amnon will hear nothing of them.

'What do you expect?' he asks, unconsciously echoing his father. 'He takes these things very hard. It isn't for me to sit in judgement on him.'

'You used to.'

'I used to do a lot of things I don't do any more.' Amnon stares unpleasantly at me for a long time. 'I used to like your face.'

That's as much of a witticism as he ever makes, these days. I don't take offence at it. I have my own jokes. Among them is my transformation, in my reports to Absalom, of this glum, bored, inert drunkard into – of course! – a sleepless schemer who may pretend in public to be remorseful and humble, but who in the secrecy of his own house exults over his past crimes, recalling them in lascivious detail, and feverishly plans further assaults upon the life and dignity of his brother.

13

Two years of this! Well, almost. Two years of Absalom's grunts and silences while he listens to my reports and the advice I give him; of Amnon's boredom and drunkenness; of speeches and sermons by the king; of idiotic scenes in the court and gossip about them. It seems improbable, I admit. But I'm afraid you'll have to take my word for it. So it was, so it has to be. If you like, if you think it will make it easier for you to accept, perhaps you should close your eyes for a brief, symbolic period; or imagine that our figures waver strangely before you, grow darker, go fuzzy, grow lighter, reappear in firm outline; or even that a small boy has come forward with a placard around his neck on which is inscribed the announcement that two years have passed. Then I'll try again.

Right. Thank you. Two years – near enough – are up. Is that better? I hope so.

Here we are then, in the throne-room once again. Or

still. Most of the spectators and actors who were here before have taken up the positions they occupied last time. Some of them have become fatter, a few leaner, some greyer, some (the youngest among them) taller; a few have died, inevitably, but I doubt if you would notice their absence; and the same is true of those who have been posted abroad, have fallen into the king's disfavour, or have simply decided they could do better for themselves elsewhere. The throne stands where it did; the drapes hang in identical folds; if there has been any fading of the blue and ochre on the walls and the gilt on the ceiling you may be sure that busy hands have touched them up so that the difference is scarcely visible. The king – his face a little more lined, his eye more watery but less bright – is on the throne; and his sons and ministers are around him. Absalom is there; Amnon is not. But Amnon so often stays away from the court that his absence is no more to be remarked upon than that of any of the others who have disappeared from the scene.

Everything, in short, is in order. For your convenience and mine we can assume that the day's business has just been concluded. Ira whispers to the scribes, who begin to gather up their scrolls. We are waiting for the king to rise from his throne and set us at liberty when Absalom unexpectedly steps forward.

'Before we adjourn,' he says, 'I have a favour to ask of the king.'

'A favour? What is it, Absalom? If I can grant it to you, you know I will.'

Absalom bends his neck in acknowledgement of this gracious remark. Then he presents his request. He asks David – 'and all the king's servants too' – to come to the party he is going to give, as he does every spring, at his estates near Baal Hazor. The occasion for the party, as before, is the festivity traditionally associated in that area with the sheep-shearing season.

Before David can answer, Absalom anticipates the objection he is most likely to make. 'Baal Hazor isn't far from here. The road is good. The weather will be clement by then. The journey will really not be too fatiguing. And it's been so long, father, since you were last in that part of the country.'

He enlarges poetically on the longing of the people in the province to see their king once more: they will, he says, speak of his visit for years to come; they will tell their children about it, describing the clothes their king wore, naming the regiment that escorted him, pointing out the villages at which he stopped to eat or rest. As for the question of accommodation at Baal Hazor, Absalom continues more matter-of-factly, he would make over his own house on the estate, it would be entirely at the king's disposal. He himself would join his other guests in the tents his workmen have already begun to put up near the house.

Absalom's speech is concluded. All very dutiful and effective; all bullshit, too. Absalom knows how reluctant the king always is to leave Jerusalem. He knows that he has in fact not done so for more than two years past. Therefore he knows perfectly well that the more he presses his request the more uncomfortable he is making his father feel.

That much is plain to everyone. David has been made uncomfortable. He doesn't want to appear impolite and unappreciative, but still less does he want to accept the invitation. He'd rather not have his routine upset. He doesn't fancy the idea of a week-long picnic among the sheep; and who can blame him? The thought of loyal hill-folk gaping at him has no appeal. (Years hence, during his abortive *coup d'état*, Absalom will chase David out of the city and rule over it for a few weeks: nothing less than that, if you please, will make the king move.) He says, 'It's most kind of you,' and 'Really Absalom, you shouldn't think of putting yourself to so much trouble'. But the look on his lined face and the tone of his voice clearly say something quite different: 'You know the last thing I want to do is to go trekking out to Baal Hazor. Then why don't you leave me alone? Why must you insist so?'

Absalom has his reasons for insisting; or rather, for wringing out of his father a firm, explicit refusal of his invitation. So he continues to urge him to come. The absurd contest or dialogue between them, in which a show of goodwill is the only weapon permitted to either, goes on. Absalom's smile is one of those in which you cannot tell where humility ends and brazenness begins; the king sits with his hand to his mouth, as if he is trying to think of how he might order his arrangements so that it would be possible for him, after all, to oblige his son.

However, after a suitable lapse of time, and to the astonishment of no one, he fails. 'You've been helping me so much, Absalom,' he says, with an air of almost petulant guile, 'you – of all people – should know just how busy I am.' A well-turned compliment, an advantage gained. 'Besides,' he adds, 'if I were to come to Baal Hazor with my entire retinue it would put you to intolerable expense. You have no idea what you'd be letting yourself in for. I agree with you, I couldn't travel without all my people; and just look how many of them there are! To inflict the whole lot of us on you . . . I wouldn't dream of it. I can't accept your invitation, no, really I can't. For your sake, not mine, I just cannot do it.'

Absalom looks suitably crestfallen; the king is satisfied

that he has found unassailably considerate and even self-sacrificing reasons for not doing what he never wanted to do. He is free now to rise from his throne. But Absalom holds up a hand to detain him.

'If you are unable to come, do you give permission to your sons to do so?'

'My sons? The princes?'

'The princes, my brothers.'

David is silent; and Absalom too. Then Absalom says, 'I've already asked them. They would like to come. But of course none of them would leave the capital without your permission.'

David suspects that Absalom has regained a point in the contest of obligation between them, though of what kind he does not yet know. 'Well, if they want to go, I won't stand in their way.'

'Good. Excellent. Thank you, father.'

Then Absalom strikes, still meek and brazen. 'I think you'll be pleased to know that I've asked Amnon, too.'

'Amnon!'

The king is not the only one in the room who says the name out loud. Before the hubbub can die down, Absalom speaks again. 'He is quite agreeable. He's eager to come. We both think that the feud between us has gone on for too long. I'm glad it's over. I'm looking forward to being his host.'

'Amnon?' the king merely repeats incredulously. 'Amnon? You've already asked him? And he has agreed?'

'Yes.'

Now Absalom is curt and monosyllabic; he has no more to say. He leaves it to the king to find the right words.

In the long, dead pause that follows, I remember the hour when David beat down Absalom, discarded Tamar, and chose to strike out in a direction none of us could have anticipated. An impressive display of faith and strength it had been: no question. But it was also, I have often thought, like the effort of a man who picks up a weight no one can believe him capable of lifting – who picks it up and is left thereafter with a strained heart. The David of two years before would not have been ashamed to announce at such a moment that he had changed his mind and was ready to go to Baal Hazor, or that he would prefer to keep Amnon in Jerusalem, thank you very much. Now he shrinks from going back on a decision he has just proclaimed; he does not dare, even by implication, to accuse Absalom of having trapped him, and of planning to do far worse to Amnon; he is soft-headed enough to hope that Absalom has at last surrendered to him and given up his hope of revenging himself against Amnon. Is he victor or loser? He looks at us as if we can answer the question for him, and reads back from our expression only his own doubt. For the first time we see that there is another possibility too: he is perhaps too weary to care how he emerges from the struggle.

'They all want to go?'

'Yes.'

'Amnon too?'

'Yes.'

'You are reconciled to him? You have forgiven him the wrong he did you?'

With a steady gaze and in an even voice, Absalom makes what could be his fiercest thrust against David; or what might be a gesture of the most complete submission to him.

'If you could forgive Amnon the wrong he did you, why shouldn't I?'

The lines around David's mouth deepen, his lips twist into a crabbed, enigmatic grimace. There is no forgiveness in it; rather, bitterness and shame, and the shadow of an amused contempt, too.

'Very well then,' he says, and his words, after his silence, sound dry and dismissive. 'If they all want to go, and if you are ready to put them all up, so be it.'

The matter is settled. Settled, it suddenly appears trivial. Yet the king's mouth works again for a moment. 'Only – '

'Only?'

'Take good care of them.'

'I will. I will do my best for them all. You may be sure of that.'

David leaves the room. Absalom follows him; and the rest of us, our eyes on the ground and our tongues ready for much exercise, troop along behind.

Your assumption is quite correct. The bearer of Absalom's fraudulent olive-branch to his brother had been your humble servant. (Absalom's humble servant, Amnon's humble servant, everybody's humble servant.) It was my final, I might almost say definitive, act of betrayal.

Actually, Amnon had made my job rather harder than I'd expected him to. After his public pleas to Absalom to forgive him, I had thought he would be embarrassingly grateful to get the message I brought him. But it didn't turn out like that. He chose instead to exhibit his talent for suspicion, his resources of offended *amour-propre*. The content, the timing, and the manner of Absalom's invitation were all found wanting in one respect or another. He objected especially to Absalom having sent him the invitation through me, instead of coming to him directly; and he demanded proof, though of what kind he didn't specify, that the invitation was not just a trick to lure him out of Jerusalem, away from his father's protection.

Since you know already that I managed to overcome his objections, I won't bore you by rehearsing the arguments I used to bring him round. But it wasn't easy. So hard did I have to work that presently Amnon fixed a moist, inflamed eye on me and asked, 'Why are you so keen for me to go, anyway? What's in it for you, Yonadab?'

A confession, rather than a denial, seemed to be in order. I made mine as ingratiating as I could.

'I suppose I'm flattered that Absalom should have entrusted me with a message like this. I mean, after all that's happened – that I should be the one to mediate between the two of you. . . . Of course I'd like to go back to Absalom with the news that I've succeeded. I can't deny it.'

I think my confession mollified him a little. I think it helped to hasten his acceptance of Absalom's invitation. But for a moment I had been greatly tempted to tell him the truth: to tell him his suspicions could not have been better-founded, and that Absalom had indeed decided the time had at last come to lure him away from his father's protection and to murder him at Baal Hazor, in the presence of all his brothers. I was curious to see how he would react; knowing the truth, would his boredom compel him to seek out the danger and excitement of the rendezvous?

In view of what eventually happened at Baal Hazor it's as well I didn't take the risk. I just went on about how important it was for him to accept the invitation, especially after having publicly implored Absalom to make just such a gesture to him; and about how much joy the news of a reconciliation between them would bring to their father. Towards the end, I suspect, Amnon would have agreed to almost any proposal I made, if only I would then shut up about it. So, perhaps one can still say that it was his boredom which undid him, in the end.

Once I had wrung the agreement from him, I talked about other subjects. Amnon stared into his empty goblet; he filled it with wine and stared into it once more, as if for purposes of comparison. Evidently he preferred it empty. Then full. Then empty. And again. Later he ceased to be capable of attending even fitfully to my words, still less of uttering any of his own. I sat watching him, while he snored and twitched on his couch. I took leave of him in silence. One last look. He was breathing; dreaming, it seemed. He would be doing neither when I next saw him.

From Amnon's living-room I then ran straight back to Absalom, losing no time, like an obedient, scurrying messenger and busybody. My good news was greeted with the usual grunts and stares; an unusual, reluctant word of thanks; a word of self-congratulation on the site chosen for the murder; one more preliminary gloat over it. And a gloat over me, too: for having let myself be pushed by him, as Absalom saw it, to the ultimate act of betrayal. In carrying his invitation to Amnon I had passed the final test he had put me to; therefore his contempt for me could be complete and unqualified.

Before dismissing me, he let me know once again that I was to come to Baal Hazor too, without fail; and I replied yes, thank you, thank you very much, I wouldn't miss it for anything. I had been to Baal Hazor with my father a few years before, I reminded him, and even without the special entertainment laid on for this year's festivities, I knew just what splendid occasions these parties of his were, and how fortunate anyone invited to them could count himself.

I had already told my last lie to Amnon; this was my last lie to Absalom. I had not the slightest intention of going to Baal Hazor. Absalom's manner of looking at me whenever we had spoken of what was to happen there had always seemed to me good reason for keeping away from the place. But I did not want Absalom to realise that I wouldn't be there until it was too late for him to do anything about it. It would be safer that way, I was sure. On his return to Jerusalem I planned to plead illness, business, my father's instructions or the king's; and to try to keep out of his reach, and that of his goons, as best as I could thereafter.

My last lies told, my last message delivered, my last secret meeting concluded, I was finished. Out of it. The rest was up to them.

I felt as one does at the conclusion of any protracted and difficult task: a mixture of relief and melancholy. Even the porter at Absalom's gate, that half-comic, half-sinister figure, appeared to me already a part of my past, to which I was bidding farewell. I waved at him as I went through the gate, and he nodded glumly, without interest.

The flare of a torch against the ruddy, rough wood of the gate, a groan of the jamb in its socket, a clatter behind me; I was in the street. I had come alone, as always, and I walked home alone, putting my feet down with care on the uneven paving. It had rained earlier, and the air was cool but sluggish, damp, slightly misty; the clouds overhead were motionless. That the broken layers of cloud were still visible, however, in an uncertain, mauve attenuation of the darkness, showed the spring to be not too far away. Amnon, I remember thinking, would not live to see the end of it, brief though the season always was.

Such melodrama! You must be sick of it. I don't blame

you if you are. What a lack of moderation and good taste everyone had shown, from beginning to end! What an extravagant series of events! Incest; rape; a girl running through the streets of a city in order to force everyone in it to stare at her and hear her screams; a father cutting off a wronged daughter; a brother planning revenge against a brother by murdering him in the sight of a crowd of guests. . . . How could people perpetrate such crudities against themselves and others? How could they commit themselves so flagrantly to the consequences of their own indiscriminate passions?

The answer that evening seemed to me plain. Princes do what we dream. Hence the extremes of violence and self-display to which they are driven, the fervour and shame-lessness of their acts. Hence Amnon's assault and the fantasies which had accompanied it; hence the brutality with which he had turned on Tamar the morning after; hence — the lot, every last turn and writhe amongst them.

Yet that wasn't all. You may put it down to the drinks I had had with Amnon, or to my relief at having completed a difficult task, or to the euphoria of having arrived at the culmination of my treachery and deceit, or to sheer megalomania on my part — anyway, as I walked through the misty, scented, silent lanes and alleyways, stone about me and stone underfoot, the further conclusion I came to was this: if princes do what we dream, then they are not our masters, but our slaves. We, commoners, fantasists, *voyeurs*, movers of furniture, carriers of messages, extras — we are free men. We can let our thoughts go where they like; in our obscurity, we are not bound by them, we are are under no obligation to them. But princes are slaves and bondsmen, compelled to act out every whim of ours, every fleeting impulse, every lewd desire, every childish dream we ever permit ourselves to have of the annihilation of our enemies and of self-exposure to our friends. Not a word breaks or bubbles from our lips as we sink into sleep or rise up from it but is a command for them, which they dare not disobey if they wish to become or remain our princes still.

Of course we reward them. We carry their messages, we move their furniture, we stand in our streets when they pass and we cheer and wave our little flags, we put their pictures on our walls and on our coins. Why shouldn't we? That is how we pay them for carrying out our wishes so zealously, for working so hard and self-sacrificingly on our behalf. A bargain, every time! And we pay them and teach them what to do, also, by telling each other stories about them, long after they are dead, long before they are born.

14

A picnic. A house-party. A *fête champêtre*. A seasonal ritual. Call it what you like. Absalom, left-wing prince and landowner, radical millionaire, aristocratic populist – call him what you like – is at home to his guests at Baal Hazor.

Tents and pavilions are pitched in the fields around the big house: tents for sleeping in, tents for washing and retiring, tents for preparing the opulent meals which, weather permitting, are eaten at long trestle-tables out of doors. The house itself is decorated with pennants and streamers, its roof is shaded with a striped awning; it could almost be just another gay, temporary pavilion. This year, however, Absalom has broken with the tradition established in the past and has brought with him many of the women of his household; the house is reserved for their use and Absalom's only.

Entertainments of many kinds are laid on for the guests. The sheep-shearing which is the ostensible reason for the whole affair is itself turned into an entertainment, with Absalom's shepherds competing for prizes given to those who prove themselves the fastest and most skilled at the job. The guests inspect Absalom's crops and flocks, which are of greater interest to them than they might be to you, for most of the guests are themselves landlords and farmers of one sort or another. There are musicians, dancers and jugglers; imbeciles and madmen who gambol about as freely as they are allowed to; necromancers who tell fortunes and claim to summon up spirits on demand; priests who follow the official cult and make their sacrifices at the ancient high place once dedicated to that other god whose name this Hazor still keeps. Horse and donkey races are organised; cock-fights and dog-fights; excursions to hunt deer in the hills.

And there are the four meals spread out every day on the trestle-tables: they are not the least of the entertainments Absalom offers to his guests. Great stews of mutton, goat-meat, venison, fish and ducks, seasoned with spices of every variety and thickened with beans and lentils; piles of bread made of wheat, barley and millet flour; side-dishes of olives and onions; bowls of this season's earliest fruits and last season's preserves – whatever the country produces or can be imported from abroad is used by Absalom's cooks. Several different sorts of ale are always available, and so are pomegranate-wines and grape-wines, and stinking but reputedly lenitive mineral waters from Hammath; there are cakes and puddings made from honey, date-syrup and milk-curds. In the rubbish-heaps down in the valley, behind the houses of the villagers, birds and dogs are so well provided for they stand eating side by side, the dogs not even bothering to lift their heads and snap at their fellow-diners. They are not the only scavengers who share in Absalom's bounty. From many miles around, far beyond the boundaries of his own estates, people come to Baal Hazor at the time of the festival in order to find odd jobs for themselves and to grab as many droppings from the tables as they can. The stewards have orders not to drive them away; their master, as the poor well know, as we all know, is a friend of theirs.

Absalom himself shares wholeheartedly in the pleasures he offers to others. He enjoys the games and dances, he applauds the jockeys and the sheep-shearers; he has time to gossip with each of his guests. His stewards sweat, worry, run to and fro, crack their voices shouting orders at servants who have eaten and drunk too much and have too much to gape at as they go about their duties. Their master remains calm and attentive. As ever, his clothes manage to combine elegance with a suitable touch of informality; and even here, in the country, his hair is dressed by his barber in styles that vary from day to day: now with a band that goes across his forehead and is looped around the back of his head; or tied back behind with a fillet; or held in place like a helmet by the application of a thick, perfumed unguent. Of all the physical advantages that Absalom is entitled to be vain about – his height, his breadth of shoulder, his regular features, his eyes, his curling lashes – he is most vain about his hair, which is exceptionally thick and of a rich chestnut colour. (Need I say it? – after his death the story will be put about that he was caught and held by the hair, his precious hair, in the fateful branches of that tree. All timorous, submissive, balding men can still derive much comfort from the tale.)

Anyway, Absalom, alive, his feet on the ground, is never more pleasant than on these occasions, when everyone around him is doing what he wishes them to do. The enjoyment of his guests is at his expense, undeniably; but by a metaphorical system of book-keeping which means far more to Absalom, it is all to his credit: the entire affair, its lavishness, the sense his guests have of being on holiday from their ordinary cares, the well-being induced in them by breathing fresh air all day and eating large meals under starlight and sunlight, the chance meetings of strangers and the reunions of old friends, the unspoken yet keen agreement among them that their presence at the festival in itself reveals them to be persons of note.

All this – to help make the visitors feel that they have indeed been lifted above their workaday selves – takes place at a great elevation, among hills even larger and emptier than those around Jerusalem. At Baal Hazor the air is thin, the light is sharp, one can see the mirage-like shimmer of the sea in the west and the haggard, female fold of the Jordan in the east, and beyond it again. There are so many rounded crests and swooping declivities, so many paths disappearing at abrupt turns – as if each path simply leaps the space between its hill and the next, where the skein-like loop of yet another track runs up towards its own point of vanishing – that hills and valleys alike appear to be engaged in a grave dance or game in which you participate merely by walking among them.

Yet they are always still: covered in the tenuous green of spring, clenched in buttresses and terraces of pallid outcrop, sprinkled everywhere with white and pink cyclamens and the tiny scarlet cups of anemones. The legend is that these anemones are given their colour by the blood of the slaughtered god, Tammuz: the lover of his sister, too, in his recurring season.

From the very beginning Amnon was set apart from all the other guests at Baal Hazor; he was favoured by Absalom with every mark of esteem and deference.

He was invited to sit at the host's right hand at the dinner-table. He was asked to act as a judge at the races and competitions, and to award the prizes to the winners. He was given a front seat at those entertainments he chose to patronise. His tent was one of the largest on the site, and was more elaborately furnished than the others, with rugs, couches, and fancy curtainings. Wherever he went he was accompanied by one or two young men – their hair cut short and their beards cut square – who were specially assigned to look after him, and who were always ready to pour him another drink, to hold him by the arm when he tripped over his own feet, and to tumble him into his bed in the small hours, after the guests had finally dispersed to their tents.

Let justice be done to Absalom. He gave Amnon all the honour due to a designated victim. He also gave his guests their full money's worth (so to speak) in the way of innocent amusements. It was surely not only to heighten the drama of the denouement, but also out of consideration for all those who had come such long distances to enjoy his hospitality, that Absalom held his hand until the last possible moment.

Let justice be done to Amnon, too. Drunk he may often have been, but he was always appreciative as well. It was frequently difficult for him to carry himself with the degree of dignity that he obviously felt to be proper to the occasion; but he did his ponderous, swaying, frowning, word-seeking best. He kept back any tears he may have been tempted to shed; he put up no unnecessary displays of humility when he was singled out for special treatment by his host; he never spoke to Absalom of the differences there had been between them. The guests agreed later, moreover, that if he did have any suspicions of Absalom or his motives, he showed nothing of them.

All the more the pity, you might therefore be tempted to say, that when the end came, as it had to, Amnon let himself down so ignobly.

I think you would be wrong. If anybody really let himself down, it was Absalom.

Having arranged for Amnon to be killed at his side, during the last dinner of the week's festivities, in full view of the throng assembled on the stage-like elevation in front of his house (strange contrast with the hole-in-corner randomness and vacancy of the place of his own death!) – having arranged all this, Absalom had to do no more than give the signal for the killing to be carried out, and then deliver to his brothers the speech prepared beforehand.

But the speech was never made. Instead of remaining rooted to their places while Amnon was done to death, as Absalom had intended them to, his brothers ran yelling with fear into the darkness and fled in a rout towards Jerusalem. Homewards. To their daddy. Whereupon, overcome with fear himself, Absalom fled like the others, but in the opposite direction: towards the sanctuary of Geshur he was to seek again, unsuccessfully, years later.

How different from the end which Absalom had anticipated to the evening's ceremonial! Had Amnon but risen like a hero to the occasion, had the murder been carried out as Absalom wanted it to – solemnly, swiftly, ritualistically, like a judicial execution performed on behalf of an authority that could never be swayed from its purpose – Absalom's expectations might have been fulfilled. His brothers might then have remained captive, unable to move from their seats or to block their ears against his speech; aghast at what they had seen yet compelled by the inevitability and ruthlessness of it; ready to support their bloodstained brother and ruined sister against any move the king would dare to make. Especially as Absalom had set up a table for his womenfolk that evening, in sight of his guests but at some distance from them: among the women, more heavily veiled than any other, was Tamar. The plan was that once Amnon had been despatched, she was to throw off her veils and reveal herself to her brothers, in a final *coup de théâtre* that would, it was hoped, lend an irresistible power and poignancy to Absalom's words.

Every detail, you see, had been worked out. But Amnon wrecked the entire scheme. His terror infected his brothers. His cowardice threw everything into confusion. The screaming, the running-about, the upending of tables and the crash of crockery, the food thrown around in all directions, the yelping of dogs, the flames from broken lamps burning in streaks on the ground, the blood in salad bowls, the lunges and pursuits between the legs of the diners, the injuries inflicted on some of them by Amnon's baffled pursuers, the sheer length of time it all took – it was these that spread panic among the guests and sent them fleeing for their tethered animals or simply running as fast as they could down winding paths of sand and stone. Anything less like an incontrovertible assertion or assumption of power it would be hard to imagine. By the end of it Absalom was left standing amid the wreckage, alone but for his executioners, who were panting for breath and already beginning to blame one another for the failure of the operation.

A failure, they called it. A disastrous failure Absalom must have felt it to be, though Amnon lay dead on the ground not ten paces from them. Now he was still. Now he made no sound. But too late, for Absalom. Who could have guessed that bored, despairing Amnon would be so keen to keep his life? That inert, drunken Amnon would be so quick to see what was coming upon him? That fat, flaccid Amnon could run so fast? Even after most of the guests had scattered, and his pursuers were no longer hampered by the crowd in getting at him, he managed to evade them again and again. They struck the air with their swords behind him and to the side of him; he ducked, swerved, ran, always gabbling and screaming either for mercy or for help from his brothers. He fell, and still they could not finish him off. He crawled under a table; he made a kind of cave for himself out of tumbled chairs; his executioners prodded and fished about beneath the table as if after a cowering, recalcitrant dog they were trying to drive out of a room. Finally they lifted the table bodily and threw it aside; but Amnon held one of the chairs over his head, clinging to it, tugging it down like a hat over his ears, while blows rained down on his back and two of the attackers tried to wrest the chair from him. The two men heaved at the chair, Amnon clung to its legs; they might have been insane bargain-hunters fighting for possession of it. Then the edge of a sword managed to find Amnon's neck; the point of a sword went through his ribs from behind. The men who had been pulling at the chair staggered back with it in their hands.

15

An ignominious end? I'm sorry. For those of you, I mean, who may have expected something more elevating. Not for Amnon or Absalom.

But an end, undeniably. The action is complete; as complete as any action ever is; it can surely be arrested here without any sense of abruptness or insufficiency. Both Amnon and Absalom have succeeded in doing what they set out to do – the one in raping his sister and the other in killing his brother – and at the moments of their success each has had to learn the extent of his failure. Now Amnon is dead. Tamar has been avenged. David still rules in Jerusalem.

And I? – if I may push myself forward at such a juncture. Well, my story is almost at an end too. But not quite. The wheel to which I have lashed myself has a little further to go before its circle is fully described. In consequence of the events you have witnessed, I have still to enjoy a moment of utterly unexpected glory.

I repeat: glory. There's no other word for it. I have still to have David, the king himself, at my feet, humble and suppliant, looking at me as if I have become the source of all authority . . . and how many people are there in all Israel who can make such a claim? You don't expect me, you can't expect me, to pass over such an event in silence.

So, rather than using this opportunity to pause, draw breath, and perhaps point a tedious moral or two, allow me to ask you to step directly into the throne-room. I know, you're tired of the place; you feel you've been there too often already. But this visit will be your very last one,

I assure you. You won't have to enter it again. Nor will I keep you long. Not at all.

For into the orderly, conventional mime of statecraft currently being performed there (or here), as on every other weekday morning – into what must certainly be Jerusalem's longest-running show – there bursts. . . .

No, not the single, sweating messenger of classical dramatic tradition whom I have been eagerly awaiting.

Our assembly is interrupted, instead, by a whole crowd of hysterical porters, valets, and grooms, servants to the princes. A dozen of them, at least. There's one of Solomon's men, another of Chileab's, a couple of Ithream's and Shephtiah's, several of Adonijah's. They are sweating, all right; they're wild-eyed, begrimed and dishevelled as well. The message they are shrieking out is that Absalom has killed all the king's sons.

All?

I know it isn't true. So do you. But nothing can stop them. All, they shout. Every one. Even little Solomon. With swords, daggers, clubs. They had seen the attack take place, they had seen the blood flow, they had heard the shrieks. Then they had run. Run all the way back to Jerusalem, to bring the terrible news to the king and warn him of what was coming upon him.

If their journey had gone on for a few hours longer, I dare say they would have convinced themselves that they had also seen the armies of the Moabites, Aramaeans and Ammonites on the march. With Absalom at their head, of course. If you're going to be scared right out of your wits, if you're going to run half way across the kingdom, you might as well do it for something worthwhile. If you're a valet and a donkey-groom, and you're going to burst into your sovereign's presence, stinking of sweat and covered in dust, you had better have a good story to tell. Besides, these gentlemen have their own ambitions (like the rest of us, Yonadab not excepted, as you will see), their own desire to be attended to as never before in their lives. And they have had one another's company for mutual stimulation all the way home.

Anyway, the howling begins even before they are finished. Only the king does not join in. Looking small, old, profoundly tired, he shrinks as far as he can into a corner of his throne. It isn't far enough. He arches his back, he slides slowly to the floor. He twitches, and begins to roll. He tears weakly at his clothes. He opens his mouth: it is wide and black inside, and no sound comes out of it.

Once the king is on the floor, the courtiers all follow his example. Their faces are lit with the not wholly unpleasurable dread that loyal subjects are bound to feel when disaster strikes their ruler. I see my father gingerly lowering himself down on all fours, and beginning to bay like a conscientious dog. Priests and officials wallow about on the flagstones in their long robes, transformed into overgrown children playing an incomprehensible game; the soldiers clutch their swords and roll their eyeballs against the approach of yet more assassins among the flailing mob that has already gathered about the door. The frenzy that burst into the room in a turmoil of cries and unfamiliar faces is now spreading into other chambers and passages of the palace; soon it will be in the streets of the city.

I manage to keep control over myself as little as anyone else in the room. Knowing what I do, I cannot resist the desire to be listened to, to be looked up at, to exert my power over the king – over the crawling, red-eyed king, his beard dusty and quenched, his fists at the end of skinny arms beating without mercy against his own head when they aren't beating on the ground. My ambition seizes me before I can calculate the costs of what I am doing.

The costs! I do what I do; and I have no chance of ever behaving differently. I try to make myself heard from where I am standing; but the people around me think I am merely adding my share of mindless caterwauling to the general clamour. I then try to get nearer to the king, and succeed in fighting my way to the group immediately around him. But even when I am no more than a yard or two from him, yelling at him at the top of my voice, he is unable to make out what I am saying; he cannot hear how unlike my words are to those of the other weepers and groaners surrounding him. He is still on the ground, so I go down on my knees, to bring my mouth as close to his ear as I can. I find myself at floor-level, child-level, the flagstones suddenly enlarged into a gleaming, uneven landscape around me, and the head of the king (when have I seen him from this angle before?) wagging and jerking like that of a small beast, a poll-goat, say, being dragged to a place it doesn't want to go to. His clothes seem to be much too big for him, which adds to the animality of his appearance; it looks as if he is trying to extricate himself from their maddening, meaningless folds.

'My lord! My lord! Your sons are safe. I know they are.'

He doesn't even look in my direction. I'm wasting my breath. What more can I do? My body answers the question for me. Without reflection, I jump on to the throne, David's seat. I am conscious at once of the enormity of the sacrilege I have committed. I know it, strangely enough, by the feeling of omnipotence that fills me; by the conviction I have of my own immunity. It is amazing, the power of that stool. King Yonadab! I have put my dirty feet on a holy place, and the holy place is now mine. For the first time in my life I possess the secret of authority. How simple it is to have self-conviction; or – which is not quite the same thing – how simple matters are when you have it! I see the bodyguards closing in on me, their swords in their hands, to punish me or to prevent the assassination they are sure I am about to attempt. But I am no more frightened of those swords than I would be if they were truly made of wood. The men carrying them will do nothing to me; they won't dare. Not when I stand where I do; not when the king stares up at me, his head no longer jerking, no recognition in his eyes, but a look of fear and appeal in them that to me is worth far, far more.

The king is on his knees before me. Yes, David, I have him there at last – my reward for how many years of humiliation and obscure treachery! Yet I know that the look of appeal on his face can change in an instant into one of murderous fury, if I allow it to. Only I have the power to restrain him. I lean forward, I say as quietly as the noise in the room permits me to, stretching and mouthing my lips over the words, 'Your sons are safe. It isn't true that Absalom has killed them all. Only one of them is dead.'

Who better than the king can recognise authority when it speaks to him? The bodyguards leap upon me, they drag me down; but David's hands are at my throat almost as soon as theirs. He holds me, he presses his face against mine. 'Tell me – ' I hear, or feel, his words against my cheek. 'What do you know? What has happened at Baal Hazor? Where are my sons?' His breath is hot and moist, as from a thermic fissure in the earth; his fingers grip the back of my neck and the cloth of my tunic, all the strength of his body in their grip; his grey, tufted ear, whorled like another kind of earth, is close to my lips.

I tell him what I know. He shakes me, trying to dislodge the words from me, and I repeat what I have said. He turns away and shouts for silence, and when his command, and the curiosity of the people in the room, who are by now aware that what they have to wail about will be affected by the exchanges near the throne – when these have produced a semblance of order, he makes me say it again. He lets me go, and makes me announce it more loudly; he cups his ears, like a deaf man, so that I have to declaim what I know for the fourth or fifth time, in a voice that I hope will carry into the farthest corner of the room.

'It isn't true, my lord, that they have killed all the king's sons. You must not believe it. Only Amnon is dead. On the day he raped his sister, Absalom swore that he would die for it; and now it has happened, it has been done. From Absalom's mouth I know this. Don't take to heart what you've just heard, my lord. Your sons are alive, they will be here at any moment. All of them – except for Amnon.'

A few minutes pass – no more – and I am proved a true prophet. The king has taken his throne once more, and has buried his face in his hands; I have been surrounded by a throng of courtiers who are less interested in the details they demand from me than in simply standing as close as they can get to the man who appears to have some secret measure of control over the king and his warring sons. Then there are renewed shouts from the door, more messengers with different and better tidings, followed soon enough by the princes themselves. Everyone weeps, the king most freely of all; there is much embracing all round. Amnon's name and Absalom's are said a hundred times, and the mention of either is enough to make yet more tears flow.

I too am embraced and wept over loudly. Not by the

king or the princes – that I would never expect, even at such a moment. It's my father who grabs me. His are tears of pride. He has seen me dominating the entire court, bringing words of comfort to the king, standing on the throne and climbing off it unscathed. I have shown myself to be a man of resource and confidence (in every sense of the word); my glory reflects glory upon him; my future and his have never looked brighter.

Ah, ambition! And success! Like my father, I am aglow, convinced that I am entitled to his embraces and the envious and respectful looks that are cast upon me from every side. Never before have I felt so virtuous, so morally deserving of the acclaim which I have never before received.

Don't we dream of peace? Of forgiveness? Of mercy?

Obviously, my dreams have not been of these, or Amnon would not be lying on the grass in front of me now. Out of my disorders, and his, and those of others, I have conspired to make the only order I am capable of; and here it is, this is what it looks like.

I stare down at Amnon's face. There is a little rusty blood between his lips; for the rest his face is less marked by the violence of his end than I expected it to be. His servants have cleaned out the scars and abrasions on his skin; as pallid now as what is around them, they appear to be of no particular significance; his hair has been brushed back from his brow and his beard has been combed. There is a curious fullness about his features, a heaviness, as though his repose were one that he has obstinately chosen to sink into. Then I realise that that swollen, petulant look on his face may be the first sign of its corruption. He lies on leaves plucked from aromatic shrubs, and branches of flowering acacia, with their tiny, yellow, fluffy balls of blossom, are arranged about his head; less as a garlanding than to disguise the smell which may come from him. His arms are folded upon his chest, and a blanket is drawn over him, up to his neck. His face is fully exposed to the sun, whose light sears even my most swiftly averted glance.

The sun shines, a spinning, silver coin or crucible, its radiance overflowing from itself, streaming down the blue arch of the sky. The hills bear their burden of rock, grass and stunted pine. The halted horses and mules swish their tails constantly with a dry, gusty sound, incongruous in the stillness of the air trapped in the pass. There are no houses to be seen, no patches of cultivation; only the beaten track – already ancient when Jacob and pregnant Rachel passed along here on the way to Bethlehem (where else?) – runs north and south. South to Jerusalem; north to Baal Hazor, the Galilee, Geshur.

I had ridden out from Jerusalem to meet the group; at my request Amnon's men halted and laid their burden on the ground to the side of the path. It was curiosity that brought me here; a wish to absent myself from Jerusalem for a while; a certain sense of obligation. But I no longer know to whom I felt the obligation when I set out. Hardly to Amnon. It must be to you. I have felt the disturbing shadow of your presence, the possibility or likelihood of it, more and more frequently, of late. I can think of no one else I am obliging by being here.

However, you mustn't mistake me. I am not suggesting that I feel a sense of disappointment or anticlimax at the sight of Amnon on his makeshift bier. Nothing could be further from the truth. Death never disappoints; it is always appropriate to the form it has taken, no matter how unexpected that may be. In life, everything is too

176

much or too little; its essence has always appeared to me disproportion, strain, irresolution. An achieved death is a different matter; it can never be other than it is. If Amnon's life was romantic, I'm tempted to say, his death is classic.

O.K. Cover him up. Get going.

But Amnon's men are not inclined to do so. Having halted, having dismounted, they now decide to take their midday rest. They carry the body into the shade of one of the trees growing above the path; they dig in their bags for pieces of bread and hard rounds of sheep's-milk cheese. Hesitantly, the leader of them offers me some of his food, which I decline. A domestic scene, a poor man's picnic. The quiet casualness of their demeanour has its own dignity. Though I have no reason to suppose they cared for him particularly, they have made it their business to bring their master's body home from Baal Hazor; they didn't wait for instructions to do so; they set about their task as naturally as they now go about preparing and eating their frugal meal. They drink from leather water-bottles; they wipe their mouths; one of them climbs up the hillside and goes behind a clump of rocks, presumably to have a shit.

'And the others from Baal Hazor?' I ask the leader of the group.

'They're coming. They're following us.'

'The women too?'

'Yes.'

'Who went with the prince?'

'Only his men.' He pauses, choosing his word cautiously. 'His soldiers.'

I'll wait then. My other victim. The obligation to meet her must be the same as that which brought me here to meet Amnon. I have nothing to say to her that I can think of, I'm sure I'll feel none of the impulsions which I stifled or which she stifled in me at our last encounter. Still, I'll wait.

Amnon's men mount their asses and mules, and begin at once to pump rhythmically with their legs astride the backs of the beasts; it looks as if it is that incessant, human effort which propels them along the path, rather than the labour of the animals. Amnon is carried on a litter slung fore and aft between two mules. The litter tilts and jerks, now forward, now back. Hooves click against stones; the men utter their usual cries. They are soon out of sight; a little later they are out of earshot. I wait where I am. I have hobbled my horse; bent like an old man over its own chest, it limps about near by, tearing at tufts of grass and blowing discontentedly into the dust.

The light of the sun becomes richer and less intense, more gold than silver, and the hills regain the colour and depth that had been drained away from them before. I grow hungry and regret that I did not accept the bread and cheese offered to me by Amnon's man. I lie on my back and doze; I listen to the calls of birds and the more insistent buzzing of flies; I listen always for the sound of another caravan approaching from the north.

At last it comes. A groaning cart or two, bouncing and staggering exaggeratedly over every stone on the uneven path; laden pack-asses; mounted men and women. I am greeted by some; stared at by all. I look for only one among them, and find her near the end of the procession, riding side-saddle on a donkey, her cloak over her head and held up to her mouth, dark eyes watchful and unabashed above. I have got on my horse once more, and fall in beside her.

We ride for some distance in silence. Then she says, 'In Jerusalem – they know what has happened?'

'Of course.'

She does not ask how her father received the news. 'They know that Absalom has gone to Geshur?'

'Yes.'

Again she is silent. Then, with a scorn that is equalled only by her composure, she asks, 'Whose friend are you now?'

I have a good answer for her this time. 'Everybody's. The king's. You'll see – you'll hear – when you get to Jerusalem. I was able to help the king, because I'd been Absalom's friend, and Amnon's friend. He was very grateful to me. Everybody was.'

She cannot know what I mean, but I add nothing to explain my words. It's my turn to put a question to her.

'Where are you going to now?'

'I'll stay with one of my brothers. One of them will look after me. And Absalom will come back, I know he will, no matter how long I have to wait.'

'You're probably right.'

We ride on. I keep my gaze ahead. The pointed, upright ears of my horse dip and rise, always at the same distance from me; beyond them, under the dust raised by the hooves that have gone before us, a strip of pallid earth constantly approaches.

'All because of you!' I suddenly exclaim. 'All of it! Yet who cares what will become of you now? What does it matter to anyone how you spend the rest of your life? Perhaps that's the biggest irony of all.'

I have spoken without malice. Or so it seems to me. So it must seem to Tamar, too, for though her stare is black and her face is blanched, she hears me without anger.

'I did my best,' she says finally. 'I did what I had to do.'

My obligation is now surely discharged. I kick my heels

179

into my horse's flanks. 'Never mind,' I say, pulling away from her, 'you'll probably outlive us all.'

I was a true prophet as far as Tamar was concerned. She did outlive us all. But about myself I could hardly have been wider off the mark. Everybody's friend, I'd called myself in talking to her. When I came back to Jerusalem I found I was nobody's friend. While I'd been away the king had called my father to him and told him that he didn't want to see my face again. Therefore, nobody wanted to see my face again.

The reasons are embarrassingly obvious. If I hadn't been carried away by the hysteria around me the previous morning I would surely have seen my disgrace coming. Probably you have already done so. *'Al pi Avshalom*, from Absalom's mouth, I'd claimed to know that Amnon was to die. But, the king had demanded of my trembling, stricken father, how had I, Amnon's friend, come by such knowledge? Having come by it, why had I kept it secret from Amnon? Even worse: why had I kept it secret from the king? How could I have dared to come forward and reveal to him, when it was too late for him to do anything about it, the secrets I'd been keeping? He didn't know which disgusted him more: my treachery, or my effrontery about it. Both were unforgiveable. Both revealed me to be unfit to hold office under him. Both made my presence totally unwelcome to him. He did not have to say more.

Indeed he didn't. Not to my father. Nor to me. What a fool I'd been! To have opened my mouth so wide would have been stupid enough under any circumstances. But like that – before the whole court – at the moment of his despair and helplessness – ! And then to be so self-infatuated as to imagine that he'd be grateful to me!

'Grateful?' I remember exclaiming to my father. 'David? To someone he's knelt in front of? Of course he'll hound me now, he'll never forgive me for it. The sooner I'm out of here the better.'

'The better for me too, I can tell you. I'm not keeping you here, am I?'

Goodbye then, dad. Goodbye Adoram and the Ministry of Public Works. Goodbye princes. Goodbye court. Goodbye glory. Back to the farm I go. Worse things could have happened to me. (The moralists among you will probably be disappointed that they didn't.) And goodbye – from a safe distance – my sovereign and liege-lord, David, king of the Jews, sweet singer of Israel, builder of Zion.

Incorrigible David! Even while driving me away from the court for having kept my paltry secrets from him, he was already giving others to understand, though without actually saying so, that of course he'd always suspected Absalom's real motives in inviting Amnon to Baal Hazor. He was also beginning to speak about Absalom in a somewhat sighing, languishing manner, appropriate to a father whose love for his son is so great he can see only the best in him. (Quite forgetting, or encouraging others to forget, that he had been ready to believe that same beloved son capable of murdering all his brothers in one spectacular blood-bath.) As for Amnon. . . . He was comforted, David said, concerning Amnon, seeing that he was dead.

A cunningly ambiguous form of words. Was it just another example of David's unrivalled capacity for cutting his losses? Or could it rather signify that he was nobly resigned, as always, to the will of God? Or did it mean that Amnon deserved what had been done to him?

I don't suppose for a moment that David himself knew what he meant. But I am sure he said it wholeheartedly, nevertheless. I tell you, he may have chased me from his court, but he remains the only man in the place I really cared for.

16

I believe there is some curiosity among biblical scholars about the identity of the gentleman they have named 'The Court Historian'. Allow me, while I can, to settle the problem for them. It was Abiathar, the priest; as a few of your scholars have already been clever enough to surmise.

A remarkable man, Abiathar. A truly original one. The founder of much more than a mere *genre* of writing. (Though heaven knows he has had countless direct imitators over the last many centuries.) Before Abiathar, what was there in the way of history? Myths and legends of every variety, many of them obscene and ridiculous; unreliable lists of the names of kings; inflated rolls of battle honours; bloodthirsty execration tablets. Abiathar changed all that, single-handed; and the consequences are still being felt in every aspect of your moral and intellectual life. Before Abiathar, I would add, the illustrious dead slept more peacefully in their caves and groves and pyramids than they have been allowed to since.

It was Abiathar, anyway, who came to me in my retirement (and his) during the reign of Solomon, and asked for my version of the events I have related to you. I told him what he needed to know, and one of his men took it all down. You may still read the story in the pages of his book.

There I remain: trapped between my past and your perpetually recurring present. Readers, breathers, onlookers, breathe on us and we tremble into life, we begin to move. Turn the page and we fall still. The choice is always yours; and if you linger over us, we know you do so for your reasons, never ours. Now that my wearisome task is once more at an end, I can only hope that I and my ghostly colleagues have served you well.

Three thousand years have passed since Abiathar put me in his chronicle. To you, it must seem a great length of time; to me, I confess, it does not. A hundred and twenty generations: that's all. If I were appearing in a theatre, as I have sometimes imagined myself to be doing, and a single representative of each of those generations were to take a seat before me, the whole lot of you together would fill up no more than a few rows of the auditorium.

It's a fantasy, of course. There is no theatre, no representatives of succeeding generations seated in orderly fashion in their rows. Only you, on your own, and these words which have been ascribed to me.

For God's sake, turn the page.